Doggone Dead

Pecan Bayou, Volume 3

Teresa Trent

Published by Teresa Trent, 2013.

DOGGONE DEAD

First edition. February 14, 2013.

ISBN: 978-1732946873

Written by Teresa Trent.

For my mother, who told me the tales of movie cowboys.

Happy trails, Mom.

Chapter 1

Zachary proudly took his new puppy's leash out of the cabinet. I held our newest member of the family, Butch, a twelve-pound weimaraner. We opened the front door and stepped out into the smothering Texas heat of late June. Zach had received Butch for his tenth birthday after weeks of parental harassment. I had relented, finally, hoping that Zach was ready for the responsibility of a dog. He promised me on bended knee that he would feed him, bathe him and walk him.

"Zach, we need to be careful walking him. He's so little, but he's strong, so he can for sure wriggle out of that collar." As if to illustrate my point, Butch started squirming as he felt the constraints of the collar and leash. He had used his entire weight to pull loose from the contraption.

"I know, mom. Don't worry," Zach reassured me, his voice reflecting the impatience he must have been feeling. He reached down and patted Butch on the head. "It's okay, boy, we're just going for a little walk."

As we headed down the driveway, Butch immediately responded to the fresh air rushing around him, and he was spurred to freedom.

"Hold on tight, Zach."

"I am. I am. He's really pulling me hard. Slow down, boy!"

Zach, arm outstretched, reached the curb of our street. Butch, blissfully unaware of the dangers of cars, plowed out on to the road, pulling Zach along behind him.

I heard it before I saw it. The low rumble of an engine going at a high speed increased in volume as I spotted a shiny red Corvette coming around the corner. A young man, biceps bulging out of his black sleeveless T-shirt, was behind the wheel.

Zach was now in the middle of the street with Butch heading toward the other side. My heart exploded as I ran into the street directly into the path of the car, swooping up Zach and causing the two of us to fall into the grassy lawn of the neighborhood playground. As I felt my knees pound into the dirt, the horn blared from the car. Its owner had hit the power windows and yelled, "Keep your stupid kid out of the road!"

I jumped up ready to yell something back that wouldn't be listed as an appropriate response by the parenting magazines when I heard Zach yell behind me.

"Mom! Butch got away!"

I turned back to Zach to see little Butch skittering through the sand under the swings and then hightailing it across the park to the other side.

There were two distinct sides to our little playground. Most of the homes on our side were three- or four-bedroom ranches, nice driveways, lawns cut by the owners and plenty of kids. The other side of the play area was a newer subdivision that had been built in the last ten years when Charlie Loper, a faded cowboy star, had sold off the land around his house in town. Even though he had acreage out in the country, the home in town became a storehouse for many of the props he used in the score of old-time Westerns he had starred in during the '40s and '50s.

Now that the subdivision had been built around the elegant structure, most of the houses on that side of the playground were two-story red brick, with short driveways and high mortgages. They were beautiful to walk through, and their manicured lawns, well-placed flowers and trees and fresh paint could be seen and envied from our side of the swing sets. Our newest family member was bound and determined to move up in the world and had headed for the shinier side of the street.

Zach and I ran after him, yelling out his name. I was amazed that anything with such short legs could move so darned fast. Butch zipped across the street on the other side of the park. I grabbed Zach by the shoulders, stopping him before he ran out into traffic for a second time.

"Look both ways!" I blurted.

Zach obediently jerked his head in both directions then up at me. I nodded back and we ran across the street together. Unfortunately, my bout of parenting gave the dog an even bigger head start on us. His little butt wiggled as his wagging tail seemed to propel him down the street. Butch looked all around, happy to be exploring. He came upon the biggest house in the neighborhood, the old Loper home, and shimmied under two giant wrought-iron gates that joined the large segments of gray brick walls surrounding the house.

"He went in the cowboy house!" shouted Zach.

"Butch!" I yelled out, now grasping the black curlicues of the gate. "Butch! You get back over here. Bad dog. Bad dog!"

Butch, not feeling the guilt, went right on taking time to pee on the historic fountain, a bronze depiction of Charlie Loper on a bucking bronco with his six gun shooting into the air. Once he'd finished tagging the statue, he happily scampered around the back of the house.

I shook the gate, the sound of metal rattling in our ears. There was a black box with a speaker and a button ner the bottom. I pushed the button.

"Hello?"

No answer.

I tried the latch on the gate. It was locked. God forbid someone from the other side of the park should get in to experience opulent cowboy luxury.

I hit the buzzer again. "Hello, is anyone in there? I'm sorry, but our dog just crawled under your fence."

Again, no answer.

Zach now slid in front of me and pushed the speaker button. "Hellllllllooooo ..." He elongated his greeting as if yelling into an empty canyon. Feeling his approach might work, he repeated it.

The black box rustled. "May I help you?" a clipped British accent came over the airway. Not exactly the voice you would expect to hear while staring at a statue of a man on a bucking horse. Whoever this guy in the box was, he didn't sound pleased we were pushing his button.

"Yes," I answered. "Our puppy crawled under your front gate, and I'm afraid he's running around on your grounds."

Silence. I waited for around ten seconds until Zach pulled at my sleeve, urging me to push the button again.

"Are you there?" I asked. "Sir?"

More silence.

"Sir? Did you hear what I said? Our puppy has ..."

"I heard you," he cut me off.

"Have you seen him?"

"No. I have not. Please leave."

I pushed the button, ignoring the black box's command. "Are there any other ways out besides this gate?"

"I have not seen your puppy," the increasingly perturbed voice said. "You are at the only entrance and exit of the estate. You must have been ... mistaken. Good day."

We had been dismissed. Zach breathed in deep and exhaled with a cry. "Where's Butch, Mom?"

"I don't know, baby. Let's walk down the block and call for him. Maybe he got out the other side somehow."

"But the guy said ..."

"I know what the guy said." Upon looking at the grounds inside the fence a second time, I noticed overgrown foliage around the house. There was also a line of rust around the fountain. From the street all you could see was the fountain and paved area around it, but once you looked inside the gate, the façade of Hollywood elegance fell flat. The grass was too high, the shrubs looked like monsters from a second-rate horror movie, and there were no flowers. They might have an uptown butler, but the place was looking ragged.

"You know, there could be a hole in the fence somewhere," I suggested. "We'll check all through the neighborhood, okay, pal?"

"Okay." Zach clutched the little blue leash with the empty collar to his chest. We called for Butch as we walked down the street. After a half hour with no luck, I knew we had to head home.

"What do you say we talk to Dr. Springer, the veterinarian? Maybe because Butch was a rescue he has a chip in him or something."

"A rescue?"

"Uh ... yep. That's the case. A lot of little dogs need homes, and we were the ones for him."

"Do you think he went back to his old home? Do you think he went to find his mom and dad?"

I was never sure if getting a dog was a good idea and had put Zach off for years. Now it was lost, and I would move heaven and earth to get it back. As we walked along, Zach talked about how the science of the microchips in dogs worked because obviously the older generation would know nothing of modern technology. As we crossed the street back toward the playground in front of the Loper estate, I heard something. Something faint.

It sounded like a tiny whimper.

I turned around as Zach ran to the swings to jump on. Could I have mistaken it for something else? I tried to isolate the sound. Zach called to me from across the park.

"Mom? Come push me." Zach stopped pushing his toes into the ground and stood up in front of the swing. "Do you see Butch?"

"I don't know. I thought I heard something."

He jumped off the swing with a thud. "Was it Butch?"

My eyes scanned the estate and up and down the street. The whimper seemed to have faded. My neighbor's dog barked on our side of the park. That must have been what I'd been hearing.

"No, I guess not. We'll head over to Dr. Springer's office."

"Can we go right now?" he urged.

"Sure," I said, glancing back. The cowboy on top of the fountain looked back at us blankly. Who lived in that house? Charlie Loper was long dead, and I wasn't really sure who lived there now. He had been known as the best shot in the West and the best tenor in Texas. Did his widow still live there? She would have to be pretty old by now. I hadn't really thought about it. I would have to ask Maggie. Whoever it was, they didn't hit the town haunts like the beauty parlor or the barbecue joint. Why live in a town if you never left your own house? I also would have picked up on a guy with a British accent shopping at the grocery store or ordering at the counter of Earl's Java.

That gray brick wall had effectively shut the rest of us out. Why did anyone need that much privacy? It wasn't exactly as if the dead Charlie had any groupies.

"Mom? Let's go." Zach pulled at my arm. "We have to get Butch back."

I looked back one last time to see an upstairs light come on in the Loper estate as the afternoon sun was fading.

*****

"Mrs. Livingston! There you are, we were just about to leave." A woman with long blonde hair and a pink T-shirt with a tiara bejeweled on the front was juggling a seven-year-old child in our driveway.

"Sorry, I didn't know you were waiting," I said as Zach pulled at my arm. Now that I had mentioned the idea of going to the vet, he didn't like the idea of waiting.

"Excuse him," I apologized. "We were out walking his new puppy and the puppy got loose. We're actually headed out again to see if we can find him."

"Man, that sucks," she offered. She held on to her daughter's hand and then swung it and smiled. The child had blonde ringlets and was wearing a fluffy blue taffeta dress. Were they on their way to a picture appointment at Super Wallie's?

"What can I do for you?" I asked.

"Oh, I'm sorry. I just wanted you to get to know my daughter, Cammy Jo."

I smiled back at the young woman, hoping she didn't realize I had no idea why I had to meet her overdressed daughter.

"Uh, hi Cammy."

"Cammy Jo," she corrected.

"Cammy Jo," I answered obediently. "Nice to meet you." A silence fell between us.

"Well, that's all. We were just wantin' to meet you before all the pageant nonsense starts in a few days. You know how crazy it gets."

A lightbulb went off in my head. I had forgotten that Rocky Whitson, my boss at the Pecan Bayou Gazette, had asked me to be a judge at the Little Miss Watermelon Pageant on the Fourth of July. I was a part of the "Watermelon Team," receiving assignments to go out to Bonnet's Farm to take pictures of the watermelon crop and judge the pageant. Once that was done I would write up something about watermelons in my column, The Happy Hinter. It was the town's effort to bring in tourists so they could stand in the death-defying heat at the parade and purchase 36-ounce soft drinks and maybe a trinket or two at the various gift shops and eating establishments around town.

"Great, glad to meet you Cammy Jo." Zach's rushed monotone signaled that he was done with the niceties. He crossed his arms and tapped his sneaker on the pavement.

"I'm so sorry, but I have to go now." I reached inside the front door and pulled my keys off the hook.

"What's he look like?"

"Pardon me?"

"Your puppy. What's he look like? Cammy Jo and I will personally find your little fella."

Was this a bribe?

"Oh you don't have to do that. I'm sure we'll find him."

Zach pushed me out of the way. "He's a weimaranaer and he's only about two months old. He's gray all over. If you find him, bring him back here."

The young woman nodded at his drilled instructions. "Yes, sir. We'll be looking for him, right Cammy Jo?"

"Yes. We'd love to look for him." Cammy Jo nodded, jerking her head up and down quickly. I could tell the idea of looking for a puppy might have been even higher on her list than dressing up and walking around in a beauty pageant.

"Thanks," said Zach, reaching up to high-five the little girl. She returned the gesture quickly, and her mother beamed at her.

Chapter 2

We pulled into the animal hospital ten minutes later. Springer Veterinary Clinic had once been a home near Main Street in Pecan Bayou. As the downtown spread out, the building became commercial, and the new owner took out the side yard and turned it into a parking lot. The light blue two-story frame house had a homey feel with its cheery white front porch. There were ferns hanging from the rails that led up to the door. Dr. Springer had thought to leave a small patch of grass on the other side. A little sign that featured a smiling beagle and the words "Be Our Guest" greeted the many canines who visited.

My nephew Danny had been working at the vet's office as a part of his supported employment program through the Texas Department of Disability Services. Danny's responsibilities included feeding, walking and playing with the dogs. Thanks to him, we found Butch. He had fallen in love with the puppy, and instead of Aunt Maggie taking him home, it was suggested that we take him for Zach's birthday. I still felt guilty for putting off the whole puppy thing, but I also wondered if I had jumped too soon. We had only had a dog for a couple of days and were already headed for heartache.

"Betsy!" Danny walked over with a broom in one hand and gave me a big hug with the other. He was only around five-foot-one, and I stood a good five inches above him. He was starting to get a little pear-shaped, probably from too many lunches of cheesy dogs and fritos.

"Did you bring Butch?" he asked.

"Butch is missing," Zach stated flatly, making me recall Joe Friday from Dragnet.

"What do you mean?" Danny backed up.

"I mean he ran off, and we need to find him," Zach said, starting to show impatience with his cousin.

"Where did he go?"

"We don't know, Danny," I said. "We thought Dr. Springer could help us."

Danny dropped the broom and started walking around the high counter to the back room. He leaned against one of the shelves filled with bags of dog food and waiting prescriptions. He yelled out, "Dr. Springer! Emergency!"

Zach and I stood there feeling the breeze of the air conditioning all around us, drying the sweat off the backs of our necks. I heard Dr. Springer excuse herself and come out of a back room.

Dr. Springer stepped out of the back, drying off her hands with a small white terry cloth towel. Her round glasses were down her nose a bit, and her blonde hair touched with grey was pulled back in a businesslike ponytail. She stuck the towel in the pocket of her white coat and stepped forward to shake my hand.

"Hi, Betsy. What's wrong?"

"I'm sorry to bother you, but we were out walking Butch in the park by our house and he pulled out of his collar. He ran off, and now we can't find him."

"Oh dear."

"I was wondering if possibly Butch had one of those chips put into him? Maybe we could track his movements that way."

Dr. Springer frowned. "Sorry, Betsy, but putting a chip in is a pretty expensive thing for a rescue dog. That's something that we encourage the new owners to do and to pay for."

"Man," sighed Zach as he sat down in a white plastic chair against the wall. He threw his hands up in exasperation slapping them down on his thighs.

"But," Dr. Springer said," we have Butch's picture on file, and we'd be glad to make up a lost dog poster for you."

"I'll help put up the posters," Danny volunteered.

"Not as good as a chip, but I guess that might work, too," I said, looking back at Zach, who now sat with his chin propped up with his hands.

"Great. I'll get Allison to print something out for you. Just take a seat and she'll bring it right out."

"Thank you," I said, walking over to take my place by Zach.

"Miss Allison will make you a picture of Butch. You'll find him. She's real good at the computer," Danny said, sitting down next to me.

"I'll tell you my secret," he said.

"What's that?" I asked. His secret could be anything from that fact that he knew all the words to his favorite song to what he was having for lunch.

"I'm in love," he said.

"You're in love?" Zach rose from his slouch.

"Yes. I'm in love."

"With whom?" I dared to ask.

"She has stolen my heart. It is Miss Allison," he said.

"That's sweet," I told him, wondering just what this might do to him if she rejected him. Even though the whole world could see he had Down Syndrome, Danny really didn't feel any different from anyone else. In our family he wasn't any different. For him, falling in love with someone without a developmental disability could spell nothing but trouble and heartache. I knew I would have to share this with Aunt Maggie.

Allison Emory, Dr. Springer's intern, came out from the back room and was pushing a piece of straight brown hair behind her ear. Allison was in her early twenties with low-rise jeans and a dog paw tattoo on her wrist. The tattoo was covered partially by a shimmering pink Hello Kitty wristwatch encircled with pink rhinestones.

"Mrs. Livingston, so sorry to hear about Butch," she said as she handed me a stack of freshly run-off posters. "Dr. Springer said we could run off twenty-five posters for you. I hope this helps."

I looked down to see a picture of Butch, sitting on a braided rug, looking up at me. He really was the cutest dog.

"Thank you, Allison. These are great. Can we put one up here?"

"Sure." She took the top one off the stack.

"Thank you, Miss Allison," Danny said.

"Danny, I think we're all finished here for the day. If you would like to go home with your cousin, you can."

"Okay. We have to look for Butch."

"I know. Good luck, guys."

Danny ran to the back and got his lunch bag while I called Aunt Maggie to tell her I was bringing him home. Allison put her hand on Zach's head and ruffled his hair.

"I hope you find your puppy, bud."

Zach sighed. "Me too."

"You never know, life's full of surprises."

"Yeah, like your dog running away."

"With these great posters, that puppy will be back in your arms in no time," she said as she went back behind the counter to get the phone.

Danny re-entered holding his Batman lunch bag tightly against his chest. "She's wonderful," he said.

Chapter 3

Five minutes later, as we descended the steps of Springer Veterinary Clinic, we had to step back for a man coming the other direction with a small beagle. The beagle seemed to suddenly become aware of his circumstances and planted his paws on the walkway.

"Excuse me," he said, looking up at us while simultaneously trying to drag his dog up the stairs. "Sunshine. Let's go," he said under his breath, sounding embarrassed at his dog's lack of cooperation.

"That's Sunshine. She's got the worms," Danny announced to everyone in earshot.

"Ooh," said Zach, backing away from the dog.

"It's okay. It's a dog thing. It won't hurt you," the man said, pulling on the green nylon leash. He tugged at the neck of his shirt collar, sticking to him in the heat.

"You want me to help you get your dog up the stairs?" Zach asked as he got behind the dog's posterior and gave a slight shove. Sunshine, not happy about the interference, scrambled up the white wooden stairs closer to her owner.

"Thanks," the man said. "That did it."

Zach grabbed a poster from my stack.

"Have you seen this dog? We lost our dog."

The man looked at the poster and then shook his head.

"No, sorry, but if I see him I'll let Dr. Springer know. Okay?"

"Okay," Zach said as he plopped the paper into his hands.

"I see you have your number on here too. If I see ..." he searched for the name printed on the poster, "... Butch, I'll call this number right away."

"Day or night," Zach said.

"Day or night." The man raised his eyebrows with a questioning gaze. "Do I know you from somewhere? I feel like we've met before. You look so familiar."

14

"I don't think so."

"I'm sure I've seen you somewhere. I don't know, maybe I'm crazy or confusing you for somebody else. I haven't lived in Pecan Bayou for very long. Would you know of a good kennel to board Sunshine? Sometimes I go out of town to visit my family in Denver and don't really want to take her on a plane."

"Dr. Springer will board her for a weekend. If you need a longer amount of time, we have Bayou Boarding located outside of town."

"Great."

"It's not too far from Bonnet's Farm."

"Where's that exactly?"

"It's out County Road 18. Go about a mile past the 'U Pick Em' sign and you'll see another sign with a golden retriever on it."

"Okay, thanks. Have you and your husband ever boarded any dogs out there?"

"She doesn't have a husband," Danny said, placing his hand on the man's sleeve as if breaking the news to him gently. "Her husband is in jail."

"Excuse me?"

"I'm divorced." I said flatly, hoping to cut off the next series of questions. I had to get off these steps. I cleared my throat. "Nice to meet you."

"Nice to meet you, too. Good luck finding your dog. I'll be sure to call if I see him."

"Day or night," Zach said again, just in case the instructions hadn't been clear the first time.

"Day or night," the beagle's owner repeated.

Chapter 4

Zach and I dropped Danny at the home he shared with my Aunt Maggie after putting up pictures of Butch on every telephone pole in town. We settled around the kitchen table, and Maggie started putting out plates for all four of us.

"Aunt Maggie, you don't have to feed us," I said.

"Yes, I do. You've been through a shock, losing little Butch. A little bit of my fried chicken couldn't hurt."

I suppose it couldn't, and one of her giant fluffy biscuits accompanied by a glass of sweet tea might dull the pain, too.

"Yeah! No frozen dinners tonight!" Zach cheered.

"Zachary, please tell your great aunt that we don't eat frozen dinners every night."

"We do, Aunt Maggie. It's just awful."

"Zach!"

Aunt Maggie placed her hands gently on Zach's shoulders as he sat in his place at the table. "I happen to know, young man, your mother knows how to cook – so save your arguments for the judge. Did you call down to the station? Judd can put an APB out on Butch."

"No, not yet."

"That must be some kind of record for you. Who'd have thought you could have a crisis without Lieutenant Judd Kelsey on the case?"

"Yeah, I know," I said, "but he's seemed a bit preoccupied with work lately. Missing puppies don't seem all that important."

"Mom!" Zach whined. "We need to get Grandpa to help. He can find anything." I thought about the many years it took him to find my now ex-husband.

"Yes, he can, but maybe we can help him out by trying to find Butch ourselves."

"That's right," said Danny between bites of crispy chicken. "We can find Butch. We just got to call him. He'll come running."

"We did call him," Zach answered. "We called and called, and he didn't come."

I thought about the little bark in front of the Loper estate. Had it been Butch, or was it the neighbor's dog? It seemed like the sound had been coming from the wrong direction. That creepy guy in the box was pretty unsettling, too.

"Aunt Maggie, what do you know about the people in Charlie Loper's old house?"

Aunt Maggie placed a bowl of mashed potatoes on the white lace tablecloth. "Oh, that house. Is that where Butch disappeared?"

"Yep," Zach said. "He wiggled right under the fence and then the man said he wasn't there."

"Really?" Maggie's eyes widened. "What man?"

"The man in the black box," Zach answered.

"Let me explain," I said. "It was a remote speaker at the gate. Whoever it was speaking to us was inside the house. Oh, and get this – it was some British guy. Do you ever remember anybody with that kind of accent around here?" I asked, sinking my teeth into a biscuit.

"Can't say that I have," Maggie replied. "The lady who lives there must be quite old by now. She's the daughter of old cowboy star Charlie Loper."

"Is that the guy on the horse?" Zach asked, referring to the rider on the bucking horse fountain in the front of the house.

"Yes, that's the one." Aunt Maggie sighed. "Oh, he was quite the star in his day. The best shot in the West. That's what they called him. His golden Colts are down at the Charlie Loper Dead Eye Museum. How long has it been since you've been in that old place?" Maggie's eyes took on a sparkle as she began her version of Charlie Loper's Texas drawl. "'Let's go get those bad guys, Ol' Bess,' he would say to his horse, and then he would jump up on it from the back end. It was a regular acrobatic miracle. I can remember going to the show every Saturday to see a double feature, and he was usually in one of the pictures. He had him a little guitar and always sang a song to the cowgirl. It was very romantic."

"So whatever happened to him?"

"Oh, he died. He had property here and a house in Los Angeles. He spent more time in California than little ol' Pecan Bayou, but who could blame him?"

"So his daughter is living in that house?"

"Probably. She was the apple of his eye. There used to be pictures of her on little white ponies all duded up in the movie magazines. What was her name?" Aunt Maggie tilted her head to one side as she tried to recall. "Libby! Little Miss Libby Loper! That's what they'd put in the magazines. Little Miss Libby Loper."

"Can we go see the white horse?" asked Danny.

"No, baby. He's long gone by now. I can't think of anyone else in the family who would still be alive. Charlie Loper's wife, Griselda, lived in the house in the '70s until she died. Didn't really see much of the daughter in those days. Strange."

"So who's the guy?"

"Don't know. If there's any residual income from Charlie Loper's films, it might be enough to support a person comfortably. I also heard he made a bundle off of some land in California. You know they did a remake of one of his movies about five years ago, and that would have brought in some big checks for her. With that kind of money coming in, he's either a boyfriend or some sort of help she's hired."

"But how can you live in a town the size of Pecan Bayou and never be seen?"

"Makes you wonder," Aunt Maggie said, "but it sounds like she's perfected it. Chocolate cake anyone?"

Chapter 5

The next day, I dropped Zach over at his friend Billy Mason's house to go swimming. They had an in-ground pool in the backyard, and the boys would wear each other out splashing around all day. While my son was busy cooling off in the blue velvet of chlorinated water, I was to spend my day in the heat and humidity taking pictures out at Bonnet's Farm. Bonnet, an old name around these parts was stressed on the second syllable, not the first.

I had spoken to Lina Bonnet on the phone, and she seemed very nice. Hopefully this interview wouldn't take too long. I had put off going for an entire week because of a slight possibility of rain, but today I was running out of time. A white sign edged in blue trim with "Bonnet's Farm" proudly painted on it pointed me down a dirt road. People drove from miles around to come and help the Bonnet family pick their crops and pay them for it.

I pulled into the gravel parking lot in front of the main building. There was a large fruit stand with baskets overflowing with watermelons, tomatoes, strawberries and cantaloupe. Next to that structure stood a white shed with blue trimmed metal handles and hinges. Behind all of that, about a hundred feet back, I could see a pretty white farmhouse with the same blue trim. What a beautiful place to get to live.

Lina Bonnet, a woman with dark shoulder-length ringlets, came out from behind the fruit stand. She was wearing a red apron that edged her jean shorts and tan legs.

"Betsy Livingston. It's nice to finally meet you," she said as she extended her hand to me.

"It's nice to meet you too," I said, not getting to finish as a now familiar red Corvette came crunching down the driveway into the parking lot. Remembering my last encounter with this vehicle, I stepped back.

"Sorry, that's Coop." She tucked her arms into her sides. "He's just getting back from town."

Coop got out of his car and threw a lit cigarette into the gravel. He ground out the glowing butt with the toe of his black boot. He looked to be in his early twenties and had a reputation for some of the wilder nights in Pecan Bayou.

"Coop," said Lina. "I was wondering if you could keep an eye out on the stand while I take Mrs. Livingston inside for a glass of lemonade. She's interviewing me for the article in the Pecan Bayou Gazette."

"Sure, I guess," he answered, reluctance in his voice. "I have some stuff do in the shed for Dad, so I'll listen for cars."

"Thanks, dear," Lina said, taking me by the arm and leading me to the house. I tried to imagine what her life must be like. A sturdy little chicken house with a fenced enclosure stood about twenty feet from one side of the farmhouse. It was nothing like the low-slung metal buildings used by the big production chicken farms down the road. The chickens squawked and scratched as we drew nearer to the house. Next to the chicken house was a fruit orchard in full bloom. Apple trees were bursting with green fruit as they were overshadowed by two rows of pecan trees. Pecan Bayou would never be at a loss for pie filling with this place.

We walked up the steps of the front porch. Pots of geraniums were situated here and there, and a comfortable cushioned rocker and settee looked like a great place for a glass of lemonade on a warm afternoon. On the other side of the house was a large oak tree with a rope swing. How many years had it been since Coop had played in that swing? About ten feet from the tree a slab of concrete held up a worn basketball hoop with a shredded net that stirred in the breeze.

"You must just love it out here," I said.

"I guess," Lina replied. "I've been here for so long I hardly ever think about it. You get used to it, like most things."

"I suppose you do."

We entered through a solid white front door, and I sighed as I felt the cool air rush over me. "Thank goodness for air conditioning."

Lina smiled. "You said it. Follow me to the kitchen. I have some recipes for you as well as some cold watermelon parfait."

"Great." We walked through a den that looked comfortable, although it reeked of cigarette smoke and another smell I couldn't place. Even though there were no smokers in the room, the stale odor lingered in the furniture. I stepped into the country kitchen with a long counter loaded with a batch of home-canned jelly. On the tablecloth sat two parfait glasses overflowing with chunks of soft pink watermelon, each placed on a bright green napkin.

"Wow, how pretty," I said. "Do you mind if I take a picture?"

"Not at all." I pulled my digital camera from my bag and snapped a couple of quick shots.

Lina motioned to a chair for me to sit in and then grabbed a small stack of paper from the counter.

"Here are the watermelon recipes I've collected over the years. We published them in a little cookbook to give out to the groups that visit. It encourages people to buy more."

"That's very smart of you. I'll try to include something about the booklet into with article. Do you have a website? It would probably be a lot cheaper just to put the booklet there so people can print it out themselves."

"No, Clay will want us to print them out and charge a dollar for them. That's what he has done with all the other little booklets I've come up with over the years."

"I see." I took a pen out of my purse. "Well, then we'll put the low price of one dollar into the article instead."

The phone on the kitchen wall rang.

"Excuse me." Lina stood and went to the phone. "Hello. She's here now. Yes ... yes ... I'll be sure to tell her that." She looked at a slim black watch on her arm. "Okay. I'll hurry ... I promise."

She placed the phone back into the receiver. "Sorry, I'm going to have to cut this short. Clay is coming and bringing in a new load of produce and needs my help. A big group of tourists is coming out in the next little bit. Is there anything else I can help you with?"

I was just digging into my watermelon parfait and the sweet taste lingered on my tongue. I wasn't sure if I was more upset with the shortness of the interview or the fact that she was hurrying up my dessert. "Um ... Rocky from the paper wants me to take a few pictures of the grounds, if that's okay."

"Sure, no problem."

I gathered up my things and looked down at my half-eaten parfait.

"Oh, please finish your parfait," she said. "I really have to apologize. Sometimes Clay gets riled up about stuff, and we all have to go along."

"That's probably why this place is so successful," I said, spooning up the remainder of the delicious pink parfait and trying not to drool juice down my chin. I obediently slurped it up and clanked the spoon into the glass. "All finished."

Lina grinned again, but it didn't quite reach her eyes. Looking into them, I saw sadness more than subterfuge. She lived in a beautiful place and ran a successful business, but still something was strange about her. As I walked out onto the porch, feeling the blanket of heat closing in around my air-conditioned body, thoughts of Lina's well-being melted from my brain.

Clay Bonnet was coming down the gravel drive steering an ancient white pickup with raised sides. He was in his late forties with a little sun-bleached ponytail sticking out of the back of his weathered ball cap. The truck was nearly full of large green melons, and he jumped out of the driver's side, pulling on a pair of tan work gloves.

"Miss Happy Hinter! Glad to meet you." He slipped off a glove and extended his hand for me to shake. "Sorry to have to be rushing you out like this, but I'm sure Lina here supplied you with all you need."

"Yes, yes she did," I answered. He still held my hand, and I tried to release it from his grip. Finally, he let go. "I'm just going to take few pictures and then I'll be out of your hair."

"Take your time. Mi casa, su casa." Somehow I didn't feel like he really meant it, unless his Spanish words really translated to "get your pictures and then get the hell out of here."

"Thanks," I turned back to Lina, now walking behind me. "How long have you lived out here?"

"Oh, about ten years I guess. Clay built the sheds and redid the barn. I fixed up the house," Lina said.

Clay took hold of my arm with his gloved hand and whispered to me. "We opened the farm to the public about eight years ago when we figured out we could make a lot more money if we had all the city folks picking the fruit. Best decision we ever made."

"That is if you like everybody in the state of Texas driving up your driveway," Coop Bonnet said as he came out of the shed. He was cleaning what looked like oil from his hands with an old rag.

"Those folks are personally paying for your college education, young man. Don't forget that," Clay added, his grip on my arm tightening.

"How can I? You remind me of it all the time."

"Well, in case you haven't noticed it takes money to live these days."

Lina stepped in between her husband and son. "All right, you two. Let's not argue in front of our guest ... our guest from the newspaper." She emphasized the last word as if I were going to run back into Pecan Bayou and start the first gossip column the Gazette had ever published. I felt embarrassed to be standing in the middle of it all, but really it was just a little father-son squabble. Nothing unusual in any family.

As if to emphasize that point, my own father showed up in his police cruiser. The Bonnets and the police had a history, and I was just glad he hadn't pulled up with the lights and siren wailing. He opened the door, putting on his Stetson and oh-so-insincere grin.

"Morning, folks."

Clay Bonnet straightened his back and smirked. "What can I do for you, officer?"

"Oh," my dad's eyes scanned the landscape, "just thought I'd take a little look around, that's all. A fellow can never be too nutritious, you know." He spied Coop Bonnet's red Corvette and walked over to it. "That is a fine vehicle, young man. I'll bet you can get some awesome speed on this baby."

I remembered telling my dad about Zach's near accident a few days ago.

"Cut the crap, you aren't here to buy fruit," said Coop Bonnet.

"Coop! I'm sure the officer is visiting us for all the same reasons as everyone else who comes out to the farm," said Lina.

"Yeah, right."

"Are you worried about my being here?" My father tilted his head to one side, his gaze fastening on Coop.

Coop Bonnet cleared his throat. "Uh, no, I don't care where you are, old man."

"Coop!" his mother repeated.

"Well, maybe I'm here not to check up on you," he turned toward me, "but my daughter."

All eyes rolled to me.

"This is your daughter?" Coop said.

"Sure is."

Lina Bonnet extended her hand as the thought of the newspaper article probably re-entered her thinking. "Well, welcome to our farm, sir."

My dad reached out and shook her hand. Clay Bonnet stood back and didn't extend his hand.

My dad continued as if the slight hadn't occurred. "And thank you very much for that kind, if not delayed, welcome. Do you mind if I look around a bit?"

"Sure, we have a fresh load of watermelons in."

He glanced over at the fruit stand. "I can see that. What do you keep in those two sheds back there? More produce?"

Clay Bonnet stepped up and put his arm around my father's shoulder and guided him toward the bulging baskets of watermelons. "Just farm equipment. The modern farmer requires more gadgets every day. Makes me kind of miss the good old days with a John Deere tractor and a gallon of gas."

I glanced at my watch. Despite all the tension in the air, if I wanted to get the pictures and turn them in to Rocky, I would have to get to work. "Well, I need to get back to town so I'll just take my pictures." I turned and took Lina Bonnet's hand in mine. It was cool on my skin. Not what I expected in the record-breaking heat of late June. "Thanks for all your help and information."

"Sure." She squeezed my hand. "Really hoping for a good write-up for our business. I do the books, and sometimes even I'm not sure how we make it, but we always seem to get by."

I stepped over to the field surrounding the house and outbuildings and took a picture as I felt the sun beat down on the back of my neck. The field held rows and rows of green striped melons, their various rounded shapes poking out from the tangle of vines. The property was edged by a thick forest of trees in the full bloom of summer. The picture would be beautiful in the online edition of the newspaper. It would have all of the beauty, and without any of the heat. That's the way to enjoy Texas.

I stepped over to get a shot of the farm from a different angle. The colors were so pretty and beautifully highlighted the old farmhouse. I walked to the side of the lot with the two sheds lining up like soldiers in my pictures. More people were walking around now, either buying watermelons at the stand or going out to the field to pick just the right one. Coop Bonnet had gone back to whatever he had been doing in the shed, and my father had gotten away from Clay Bonnet. If I had to interpret my father's actions, he was definitely snooping around Coop Bonnet's car. What was he looking for, the blood of his last victim? I snapped another picture of the people milling around, hoping it would lead to more sales for the farm.

"Excuse me? Aren't you Mrs. Livingston, the Happy Hinter?"

Behind me a woman stood with her left shoulder slightly stooped from an oversized red leather purse. Was she planning to secretly pop a watermelon in that thing? Had she already? Next to her was a small girl decked out in a pink satin dress with black sequined seeds sewn to the bodice and a green taffeta ruffle. Although her head moved as she took a pose, her hair frozen in a massive heap of Final Net hair spray did not.

"Well, isn't this a surprise?" the woman said. "I'm Amanda Harris, and Haley and I were just out getting some glamour shots for the pageant."

Another pageant parent. Funny how I kept running into them.

"Yes, it is quite a surprise," I replied.

"This is just wonderful. As long as we have you here, let me get your opinion on the talent Haley will be performing at the Miss Watermelon Pageant." The woman leaned down and whispered in her daughter's ear. The little girl broke her pose and then cleared her throat. She smiled, showing a row of fake teeth fitted over her own childhood toothy gaps.

"And now a number from old Broadway," she lisped – and then proceeded to belt out "Thummertime" from Porgy and Bess. She was heading into the second verse when I stopped her.

"Uh ... Haley. That is just wonderful, and I'm sure it will be great for the pageant."

"You think so?" said her mother. "We were wondering if maybe we needed to put some dance moves in, you know like this?" She put her bag down on the ground and began to do some jazz hands, stepping side to side.

"I really couldn't say," I said. "I'm sure you'll come up with something great. So sorry, I didn't realize what time it is. Have to get going. So nice to meet you."

"Nice meeting you and getting this special time together."

"Yes, well I'm actually out here taking pictures for the paper for a spread we're doing on the watermelon festival, so I'd better get back to work."

"Pictures?" She pushed her little girl in front of her, the red purse now a backdrop for precious Haley. "Well, then take one of my Haley so that the people in the town know we're out here supporting the local watermelon economy."

"Oh, no need for that. I think I'm just supposed to take pictures of the grounds and a few of the watermelons."

"You want to promote the pageant as well as the festival, now don't you? This is the perfect way to do it." Her voice lowered slightly, "Take the picture."

Feeling a little intimidated by her tone I raised my camera, "Cheese, Haley."

"No, no, no. You can't take her picture standing in front of me." She looked around and spied one of the two sheds. "Over there against that nice white background." She tugged both me and her daughter to the white shed twenty feet over from where we were standing.

She posed her daughter up against the shed leaning slightly to the side with one toe pointed. The little girl turned on a fabricated smile, and I snapped her picture."

"Great, I got it." I hoped she didn't ask to see it on the camera as I also got part of the other shed and my dad in the picture.

"Wonderful, I can't wait to see it in the paper. Where can I get extra copies?"

"Well, there's no guarantee which picture my editor will pick for the article."

"Oh, don't you worry, he'll pick her. Oh, and could you email me a copy of the picture as well? I would love to add it to her portfolio, you know." She rummaged through her red bag, pulling out a small business card that read, "Amanda Harris, Manager/Publicist/Parent of Haley Harris."

"Sure." I took the card and quickly put the camera back in my bag before she plopped her daughter somewhere else for a picture.

"Back off, cop!" I heard shouted from the other side of the shed. "This part is not open to the public," Coop Bonnet said.

"And why is that?"

"Because it's none of your damn business, that's why." Lina and Clay Bonnet came running from the fruit stand.

"Lieutenant Kelsey, I think your field trip is now officially over."

"Whatever happened to that good old farm folk hospitality?"

"You gotta be kidding me with that good ol' boy grin. You're just looking for some reason to take me in," Coop sneered.

"That's enough, Coop." His father interrupted the ranting of his red-faced son. "Be on your way, Lieutenant Kelsey."

"Certainly, but just know the next time I come back I'll be bringing a search warrant with me." My father leaned down next to the car and picked up something that was hanging out of the door. "Oh my," he said. "Look what I've found here in plain sight." My father opened the door and pulled a small baggie that looked like it was full of some sort of moss, but it wasn't moss. There was also a piece of light blue plastic in the bag that looked like it had been torn off of something.

"Coop, I'm going to have to bring you in for possession."

"It's medical marijuana. I have allergies."

"That's too bad seeing as we don't allow marijuana for medical reasons in Texas." Coop looked down and shifted his feet.

Clay Bonnet stepped between them. "This is ridiculous. I'll have a lawyer on your ass before you can pull out of the driveway."

"I'm sure you will," my dad answered. He pulled out his cuffs and put them on Coop Bonnet and led him back to his cruiser.

Clay Bonnet took off his ball cap and pushed the sweat out of his eyes. "Don't worry, son. We'll have you out in time for supper."

Chapter 6

Reasoning that my Aunt Maggie would want to know what just went down at the Bonnet farm, I made a quick stop at her house before picking up Zach.

Maggie was stooped over a flowerbed pulling weeds. She wore a floppy straw hat, and when she straightened up to greet me her face was a deep red.

"Aunt Maggie, it's too hot for you to be out here weeding. Let's go inside."

"You're right, but these weeds have been bothering me for days. I just had to get out here and give 'em a yank. Glad you're here. Time for a break. I have some fresh-made lemonade in the refrigerator. Some of my lemons were ripe." Aunt Maggie pulled off her hat and placed it on a peg by the door. I followed her to the kitchen, walking by a wall of pictures that encompassed Danny's life so far. In one picture he was six catching a fish with his dad, in another he was getting a medal in the Special Olympics.

"Here we go, Betsy." Maggie placed a glass of lemonade on the kitchen table. "What brings you by?"

I pulled out a chair as she poured her own glass and ran her wrist across her perspiring forehead.

"It's a couple of things. One concerns your brother, and one concerns your son."

Maggie pulled a chair up to the table. "Oh, my word. Well, let's start with Danny."

I nodded. "We had an interesting conversation at Dr. Springer's office yesterday."

"Go ahead." Maggie raised the glass to her lips.

"He told me he's in love."

Maggie put the glass down. "He already told me."

"What are you going to do about it?" I asked.

"I don't know. I suppose I'll just let nature takes its course."

"What if he gets hurt?"

"I know. I know it's a problem. But how can I tell him he can't have a crush on her? How do you think he would react to that?"

She was right. The minute you told Danny he couldn't have something, he had a hard time understanding. Allison was just a lovely young girl with a good heart. My cousin misunderstood her kindness as romantic affection. Even with Down Syndrome, Danny was a young man with all the same hormones as other young men his age.

"When did he tell you?" I asked.

"Oh, a few days ago, I guess."

"Didn't he have a girlfriend from his class?"

"Yes, and as far as I know they're still an item."

"Grass is always greener."

"I guess. So how was your trip to the farm?"

"Funny you should mention that. It brings me to the second reason I came by," I answered.

"What happened?"

"Dad happened. He was snooping around while I was there."

"Snooping?"

"He was suspicious of Coop Bonnet and his little red Corvette. He was being so nosy they were about to kick him out. He said he would come back with a search warrant."

"He didn't already have one?"

"Guess not."

"Doesn't he watch Law and Order?" Maggie scoffed. "That Bonnet guy and his son. What rednecks."

"Yeah, well, he's threatening to sue now, and I was starting to like Lina. She seemed really nice. Then, Officer Judd all of a sudden found a bag of pot when he was leaning over looking at the Corvette. That was enough to arrest Coop. Not my favorite way to get a story for the newspaper."

"You're right. You'd think my brother could do his drug busts at a more convenient time."

"You think? On top of everything else, I'm being stalked by these pageant parents. A mom from the pageant showed up and had her daughter start performing a Broadway number for me. What would happen if the other parents found out that this little girl finagled extra time with the judge? I'm beginning to think I never should have volunteered for this thing."

"You volunteered?"

"Good point. No I didn't, but now I'm knee-deep in watermelons and little girls."

"And their mamas."

"Right."

"A stage mother is the most over-focused, well-meaning, crown-pursuing animal out there, darlin'," said my aunt, "and you just found yourself in their sights. You might want to stick to home until the pageant."

"If I only could. We haven't heard anything about Zach's dog yet."

"Oh dear. I hope the little fella didn't get himself run over."

I rolled my eyes. "I hope not too, but I have this one thing that's been bothering me."

"What's that?"

"Well, and this is going to sound strange, but what if ... maybe ... that British guy at the Loper mansion lied to me?"

"Why would he lie to you?"

"I don't know, but I can't get it out of my head. I just keep hearing that little bark."

"That's crazy. Those people have plenty of money to buy their own dog."

"Not if they don't ever leave that house."

Maggie tipped back her glass, getting the last drops of the cool, sweet drink. "So, what do you say we go and visit just to see if they've seen the dog? What could it hurt?"

What could it hurt? I knew she was right. Just a friendly little visit to see if maybe, just maybe, they stole our dog? Worked for me.

"Would you come with me?"

"Sure. I'd kinda like to see inside that fence, anyway. It could be a pretty hot topic down at Ruby's." She was referring to the gossip epicenter of Pecan Bayou, Ruby Green's Best Little Hair House in Texas. More than one perm had gone too long and fried while Ruby was in the middle of one of her broadcasts. I always chose the basic cut, light on the latest news.

*****

Ten minutes later, Maggie and I stood before the ominous black box in front of the Loper house. "Place looks a little run down," Maggie said as she fingered some peeling paint on the wrought iron.

I pushed the button on the box. "Hello? Is anyone there? This is Betsy Livingston again, and I was wondering if you had seen our little dog? ... Hello?"

Maggie grasped the metal gate and pulled her head forward to see into the courtyard in front of the house. "Pretty cheesy statue of Charlie Loper." Her eyes brightened as she chirped out an old tune, "It's Charlie Loper, the best shot in the West." Her voice was reminiscent of an old radio announcer. She broke into song again. "Giddy-up little cowboy, the sun's going down. Giddy-up little cowboy, we're goin' to town."

"Hello?" Still no answer. I decided to do my best Texas taxicab whistle. I pushed on the button and, putting my mouth near the speaker, produced a shrill whistling sound into the box.

I heard a slight scuffle and hoped to finally be face-to-face with the man in the box. From around the other side of the cowboy fountain, a tiny yip sounded out, then another. Butch's little paws made a clicking sound as he came bounding up to the fence.

"Butch!" I exclaimed as the little dog tried to triple his own height in puppy leaps. "Butch! We found you at last!" I put my hands through the wrought-iron gate to pet him. He barked and bounced off my extended arms.

"Wow. I have to wonder if he's been here all along."

Aunt Maggie gasped. "I have to wonder what Butch just left all over your hands."

"What?" I said, pulling my hands back in to examine them. I backed away from the fence. My hands and arms were covered in something brown and sticky that looked like blood. Butch continued to bark and jump on the other side. There were little paw prints of the stuff dotting the inset stones from the fence to where he came around the fountain. I went to the gate handle and jiggled it. It was still locked up tight.

"I'm thinkin' somebody's real hurt back there, Betsy. We have to get in somehow."

She made it all sound so simple. I shrugged. "And how do you suppose we do that with the gate locked?"

"You're young and have two legs a lot longer than mine. I'll hoist you up."

I put my foot in her hands as she boosted me over the wall. With Maggie's low center of gravity she could only raise me a few feet off the ground, and I had to pull myself up to the top of the wall. I felt the skin under my shirt scraping on the uneven stone barrier that surrounded the house. I hoisted my leg over the wall and bounced down into an overgrown bush. More scratches. As I emerged from the shrubbery, Butch came over and jumped into my arms.

"Good boy, fella. Let's see what all the mess is about," I said to him, trying to forget the possible bodily fluid he was covered in. He craned his neck toward me and licked me on the cheek. Holding on to the puppy, I walked up to the faded ranch house and used my fist to bang on the door.

I thought I heard a muffled noise in the house and waited, but after twenty seconds or so heard nothing. If someone was in there, they were choosing not to come to the door.

"No answer," I called as I turned back to Aunt Maggie still waiting at the fence. My eyes shifted from her to a crumpled form on the other side of the fountain. On the ground lay a man with silver hair matted with blood and whose right cheek was now mashed into the pavement. His black velvet bathrobe was partly saturated with blood that had run down to a pair of well-soled black house slippers, and there was a wide circle of blood plastering his white-and-gray striped pajamas to his chest. The heat of the Texas summer was beating down on him as the familiar buzz of flies reached my ears.

Chapter 7

"Aunt Maggie, call an ambulance!" I yelled around the fountain. "There's an injured man back here."

"Oh Lord," I heard her say on the other side of the fence.

I looked back up at the ancient home looming behind me. Was the killer still inside? Where there more bodies? I turned back to Maggie. "I should probably check the house."

"I don't know, Betsy. It might not be safe. Why don't you try to get the fence open from that side?"

"Okay. I started toward the gate, putting the wiggly Butch back down on the blood-stained ground."

"You there!" A voice from up on high shouted out to me. "You there, girl!" An old woman teetered out of a window on the top floor of the house. Strands of her white hair fluttered in the wind. Her scrawny body, clothed in a faded pink negligee, was balanced on the windowsill. If she leaned just a little further out, she would be joining the robed man by the fountain.

"Ma'am, get back inside. I'll come up."

"Well, I should certainly hope so, and watch your tone with me, girl," she slurred.

When I tried the doorknob, the door opened easily, and thoughts of a crazy bloodthirsty intruder re-entered my mind. What if someone was hiding in the house getting ready to do in the old lady? Would they find my body alongside hers? Butch scampered behind me, my able-bodied ten-pound canine protection against a killer. Hopefully he had all of his puppy teeth. I could already see my next Happy Hinter column: Bloody paws in the carpet? Try putting your dog out BEFORE you commit murder next time.

As I made my way through the downstairs, I had to maneuver around cardboard cartons scattered about. Were they moving? Was the

British guy the crazy lady's husband? I weaved my way through boxes stacked upon boxes and finally found a stairway.

"Grayson! Get up here. I need you," the old lady shouted on the next level. She strung out the last sentence in an almost playful way. She repeated the sentence again, and as I entered the room, she was crawling up on a window seat. As she was about to put a leg out the open window, I grabbed her by the shoulders and pulled her back inside the bedroom. The smell of the room hit me first. It was a mixture of stale perfume and unwashed linens. The old woman pulled away from me and headed back to the window.

"What?" She had spotted the man by the fountain. "Grayson, what are you doing sleeping down there? I don't pay you to sleep on the job. Get up here, Grayson."

"Ma'am. You need to come away from the window."

"Says who?"

"Says me, um, Betsy." I stood and squared my shoulders, aware that my clothes were now stained with blood. I pulled her back again.

"I'm not going to fall out any damn window. I have to wake Grayson. Didn't you see him? And what's that all over your uniform? Where is your standard of cleanliness, girl? I'm going to have to call the agency."

I sighed, reaching for patience within me. "It's blood and yes, I saw Grayson. He's ... hurt. We've called an ambulance."

"Hurt?" She bolted from me again and ran back to the window seat she had been perching on. She sobbed through the billowing curtains. "Grayson, darling! Grayson, can you hear me?"

Butch wandered in. Navigating the stairs proved to be difficult with such short legs. He put his front paws on the window seat where the old lady sat crumpled. "Scout! Ooh, my baby. Go help Uncle Grayson."

So the woman *had* taken Zach's puppy. She and the dead guy, Grayson, had been hiding him all along.

"His name is Butch, and he's my son's dog."

"It is not. His name is Scout. I should know because I named him myself." She picked up Butch and stumbled across the room to the unmade bed. "Off with you now. We don't need the house cleaned today." She crawled into bed, pulling the covers up over Butch. His wriggling form could be seen under the dingy white sheets. I hated to think about the mess he was making with his bloody paws and fur.

A siren wailed outside the window, and flashing lights were blinking up against the gate. I glanced out the window as the paramedic stepped out and Maggie gestured to the second-story window. One of the paramedics rattled the locked gate and couldn't get into the crime scene. He shouted to me in the window.

"Ma'am. I need to open the gate to get in and give assistance." He stopped and repeated his question in a slower pattern. "How do I open the gate?"

I turned back to the room's occupant. "How do they get the gate open?"

"Grayson will get it for them."

"Grayson can't help, Ma'am. He's the one who's hurt. How do they open the gate?"

The old woman turned toward me. "Grayson keeps the key to the gate. Check on his desk."

"Where's that?"

"You've cleaned it, you should know by now. I can't believe he even hired you. My head is beginning to hurt." Butch crawled out from under the sheets, landing with a plop on the floor. Her eyes fluttered closed.

Looking around, it didn't seem like they had hired anyone to clean the house in quite a while. Butch, now free from his captor, ran around the room with his tail wagging.

"Okay, fella. Where's Grayson's office?" A man's voice came over a speaker down the hall.

"Hey Betsy, are you up there? This is Orley from the Pecan Bayou Emergency Unit. We need access to this gate."

Following the voice, I found a bedroom that had been converted into an office. More boxes were scattered everywhere, some open and some still sealed. China, vases and electronics peeked out of their bubble wrap as if the recipient took one look and shoved them back in the box. Shuffling through papers on the desk, I uncovered a little red light on a speaker box. I pushed the button underneath it.

"Hello?"

"Betsy, we need to get into this gate. Can you get down here and open it? "

"Hi, Orley." Like so many people who worked with my dad, Orley Ortiz was like one of the family. His kindness and patience with people in crisis never failed him. Getting through a locked gate was a little tougher. I continued, "I climbed over the fence. I'm looking for the key right now."

"Copy that. Maybe we could climb over to get to him while we wait."

I searched through mounds of papers, most of them sales orders, bills and payment due notices.

"Betsy," Aunt Maggie's voice came through the speaker. "Be careful. Are you sure you're alone?"

I had forgotten about that threat. Looking behind me briefly, I returned to the phone. "I think so. Just me and the old lady, right now."

"I'm thinkin' that's got to be Charlie Loper's daughter. Did you get her name?"

"Not much more than crazy lady hanging out the window at this point."

"Oh, Betsy. They're over the fence ... I think they just found a key in the man's pocket."

"The man's name is Grayson if you didn't hear it being yelled out the window."

"Is that what she was sayin'? They're gettin' the fence open. Can you get out of that house?"

"Tell Orley I think the woman up here probably needs medical assistance as well."

"Is she hurt too?"

"Nothing that a cup of coffee and cold shower wouldn't solve. I don't want to leave her and have her fall out of her bedroom window."

"He's on his way up. Judd and George just pulled up."

I made my way back to the bedroom where the lady now softly snored. On most of the walls were pictures and movie posters featuring Charlie Loper, the best shot in the West. His cowboy-clad image smiled at me as he rode astride a bucking horse up against a sunset. He was singing to a beautiful señorita whose black eyes reflected back true Hollywood love. His presence was everywhere. Butch scrambled back up on the bed, but the woman continued to sleep. I went back to the window and looked out at the body of Grayson, now surrounded by Pecan Bayou's finest. George Beckman, the other working officer on our little police force, was writing things in his little black notebook. A woman I didn't recognize in a police uniform was now standing at the gate. Had Chief Wilson broken down and hired a new police officer? Her hair was pulled back in a straight brown ponytail, and in her gloved hands she held a camera. From behind her, my dad, Judd Kelsey, emerged. Maggie pointed up to the window, and he shook his head at me.

It had been more than a year since I stumbled over a body in the Pecan Bayou library. I had to admit I seemed to have a knack for finding bodies. Maybe I was the human form of a cadaver dog? He had to be so proud. He folded his arms across his chest and grimaced at the window.

"Girl, bring me some tea, won't you?" I jumped. She was awake.

"Ma'am. Can you tell me your name?"

Her eyes widened. "I'm the daughter of the great Charlie Loper. Didn't you recognize me? My photo was all over the movie magazines riding my horse, Snowy." Her eyes misted for a moment as she focused on a photo on the opposite wall of a little girl riding a horse. "Oh, Snowy. I miss you still." She sighed, and her eyes darted back toward me. She returned to scolding the help. "I'm surprised you didn't know that already. Didn't Grayson tell you anything? I'm Libby Loper, you simple girl."

"Sorry, Miss Loper. I didn't know."

There was a soft knock on the door. "Betsy?" Orley Ortiz came in, taking off the stethoscope he had around his neck. His blue uniform shirt was already showing patches of sweat.

"Good, the police have arrived," Miss Loper said. "I want you to arrest this woman for breach of contract."

"Excuse me?"

"She refuses to clean," she said, pointing a scraggly finger my way.

"I'm sorry, ma'am. I'm here to give you medical help. You hired this lady to clean your house?" A smile inched into the corners of his mouth.

"Arrest her."

"How much have you had to drink today, ma'am?"

Libby Loper's eyes grew wide. "I beg your pardon! You obviously don't know who I am. How dare you ask such an impertinent question."

"I know exactly who you are, Miss Loper. I ask because I'm concerned for your safety."

"Well for your information, Officer Redneck, I haven't had anything to drink today." Her words slurred slightly. "I'm a tee-tot'ler."

"Betsy?" The speaker from down the hall beckoned me.

I ran back to it, Butch at my heels. "Yes, Aunt Maggie?"

"They have some questions for you down here. Can you come down?"

"Sure." I went back down the hall and stuck my head back in Libby Loper's bedroom.

"Will you be okay, now Orley?"

"Not a problem, Betsy. Better get back to that cleaning." He grinned.

Chapter 8

The body of Hunter Grayson was now steaming as the sun heated up the paved stones. A putrid smell was starting to rise, and I covered my mouth as my father stood quietly, hands on hips, looking at the scene. I knew he was trying to see every little detail of the crime. He was in his zone of observation. The policewoman with the camera was now snapping pictures at what looked like every cobblestone in the courtyard. Butch ran ahead of me toward the gate.

"Betsy, you're going to need to get that damn dog out of here. He's destroying the crime scene," Dad said. I picked him up and handed him through the fence to Aunt Maggie.

"Sorry," I apologized, "but think about it, he is your only witness."

"We'll be sure to polygraph him later."

"Zach will be glad to see him," Maggie said, still standing at the gate.

George came up, notebook in hand. "Betsy, did you see anything? Did you see anyone leaving the scene?"

"No. We came to see if the people who lived here had seen our dog. Butch came running up to us, and that's when we saw the blood all over him."

"So how did you get in?"

"I climbed the fence."

George looked over at the six-foot wall. "That's pretty high for you, Betsy."

I glanced at Aunt Maggie. "I had help."

Maggie suddenly looked down at the puppy as if to hide her corrupting influence.

"Do you know this man?" My dad asked.

"I think he might have been the guy we talked to over the intercom, but I never actually met him."

George pulled a plastic bag out of the dead man's pocket. Inside was what looked like some sort of moss in a blue plastic wrapper. "See any more of this inside?"

"No. What is it?"

"Looks like Mr. Grayson here was a pot smoker. Let's see if there's any more in the other pocket."

"You think this might be drug-related?" I asked.

"Well, somebody sure did him in. I'll have to leave it up to the coroner, but I would say he was hit with something. Something big and heavy."

"Grayson!" The scream came from Libby Loper as she came out of the house holding Orley Ortiz's arm. "Who hurt my Grayson?" She turned to my dad, waving a finger wildly in his face. "Ossifer. I expect you to investigate this to the highest extent. This is murderrrr mos' foul."

"Yes ma'am, that's exactly what we're going to do," he said, tipping his Stetson.

"My father had to solve a murder in one of his movies. 'Murder Under the Western Skies,' it was called. It was the ranch foreman ... Oops, I guess I spoiled it for ya," she cackled as she leaned her head sideways, glancing at the body.

Orley attempted to maneuver her around the splotches of blood and the activity that surrounded the dead body of Hunter Grayson. The policewoman with the camera came up behind me.

"Excuse me, could I get you to move over there? I need to get a shot of this hair on the ground."

"Oh," my father said. "Betsy, this is Elena Morris. She is our newest officer and will be acting as our crime scene photographer today."

"Didn't know Pecan Bayou had room for one on the payroll."

"We don't, but she is Judge Patterson's stepdaughter, and somehow the finance part worked itself out."

"Okay." I nodded my head. "I'm Betsy, Judd's daughter. Nice to meet you."

"Uh-huh," she said, still focusing on the something on the ground. She brought a flashlight out of her bag and focused it on the minuscule element. It was a hair. Once it was properly lighted, I could now see it even on the dark surface.

"Wow, you're pretty good at this."

"I should be, I did it in El Paso for three years. I got my share of crime scenes on the border."

"I'll bet." I moved out of the way. Her dark brown hair was pulled back in a functional ponytail. Everything about Elena radiated a no-nonsense approach to life.

As I stepped back, I noticed what looked like a short pedestal of some sort behind an overgrown bush. On the ridge around the top where a plant would have stood was an unmistakable bloodstain.

"Dad, maybe you ought to see this."

He came over, and upon seeing the pedestal, pulled me toward the fence. "Time for you to go, and thank you for finding what might have been the murder weapon. If you keep pointing stuff out, though, we'll have to put you on the payroll. We're going to be here for at least another hour. I think we have all we need for now. I'll give you a call when I come up with more questions."

"Great. I'm ready to get all this blood washed off."

Aunt Maggie had been joined at the gate by various neighbors peeking in around her. Donald Simmons, the now-retired owner of Simmons Hardware, stood with his fingers in his belt loop. He shook his head up and down as if he expected all of this to happen.

Maggie leaned across the opening in the gate. "George, I think you need to hear what Mr. Simmons here has to say."

George came over, flipping open his notebook like he'd been practicing this move at the station. Mr. Simmons peered into the notebook, his round glasses magnifying his eyes to a bug-like appearance. "I heard a scream last night, probably around 10 or 10:30. I live in that house over there." He pointed to a two-story frame house to the left of Loper's courtyard. His upstairs windows had a direct view of Libby Loper's house and yard. "When I looked out, it was kind of blurry, but I think it was some cowboy."

"We are in Texas, sir. We do have that type running around."

"Not that kind of cowboy, an old-timey one. Like Roy Rogers or something."

"How could you tell? It was dark out," I asked.

"He had on a vest that had some of them sparkly rhinestones on it. It reflected off the streetlight when I looked out, then he just vanished out of sight. Darnedest thing I ever saw."

Maggie jumped in. "I'll need to call Howard, the head of the paranormal society. It sounds like the ghost of Charlie Loper, back to avenge his daughter."

The old man looked at her and pushed up his black-rimmed glasses. "Holy cow, I never would have thought of that. By gosh, you might be right!" He slapped his knee, then his tone took on reverence. "Charlie Loper rides again."

Chapter 9

Aunt Maggie offered to pick up Zach when she got Danny from his job at Dr. Springer's vet clinic. In the meantime, I brought Butch home and hosed him down and then washed him with doggie shampoo using my rubber gloves. I was surprised the Pecan Bayou Police didn't ask to keep him for evidence. Glad to be home, Butch ran all over the house rediscovering his turf. Zach would be so excited to see him.

Knowing I still had an hour and had not turned in my pictures to the Gazette, I put the SD card from my camera into my computer. I could email the pictures I had taken of the Bonnet Farm and type up the watermelon recipes. I didn't think Rocky would like my clumsy Little Miss Watermelon shot. My photography skills weren't all that great, and many of the pictures I sweated out in the heat to get would end up victims of the delete key. Nevertheless, I did what he asked me to do. My assignment was the recipes and the pageant, and Ruby Green was going to try to put something in her gardening blog about raising watermelons. It was amazing she even had time between all of the conditioning treatments she was having to do to combat the frizz caused by the heat and humidity. I wondered if she knew anything about Libby Loper. If there was any news to be had, she would be the one to have it. Some of her sources were better than the microfiche in the history section of the public library. People would get all relaxed sitting in that chair having their head massaged with sweet-smelling soap, and it seemed to loosen their tongues. Secrets would start leaking out in a room full of nosy women. Big mistake.

I included recipes for berry watermelon smoothies and watermelon lemonade and emailed it all off to Rocky. I picked up the phone and called the Hair House.

"Miss Ruby? What do you know about Libby Loper?"

"Now that takes me back." She snapped her gum on the other end of the line. "Libby Loper," she said slowly. "Poor little rich girl. Libby Loper."

"Really, that's how you remember her? What do you know about her?"

"Haven't seen her in years." She went on as if I hadn't interrupted her. "She used to get her hair cut and curled about once every two weeks when she was in town. She was married three, maybe four times, but that never seemed to work out for her. They were all in it for the money. Her daddy left her a big wad of good ol' cowboy cash. I guess his movies and trinkets brought in quite a bit too, especially after they did a remake a few years ago. People wanted that original Charlie Loper stuff. Real retro, you know."

"So you hadn't seen her in years?"

"No, can't say that I have. Hold on a minute, honey." I could hear the "ssst" of the aerosol spray can as it coated yet another big Texas hairdo in a blanket of hairspray. Miss Ruby then told her victim to pay Gigi up at the counter and have a real nice day.

"Okay, darlin', I'm back. So why are you asking about Libby Loper? Did she die or something?"

"Um, no. Well, almost, I guess. I'm not sure just how much I should be talking about at this point." I heard Miss Ruby suck in air on the other end. Her overexposure to aerosol had done nothing to her nose for news.

"You can tell me, darlin'. We're like family, you know."

"I know. Miss Ruby, when Miss Loper came into the Hair House, did you notice if maybe she was ... taking drugs or drinking?"

"You mean was she high?" Ruby laughed. "Only on herself, dearie. She would give me this bull about how they did her hair when she was in Hollywood. She had the same hairdresser as Katherine Hepburn and oh, what a wonderful job *she* did, a real professional. Made me feel like the lowest wart on a toad, it did."

"So she didn't seem inebriated or anything."

"She was as sober as the preacher on Sunday morning."

"Okay, thanks."

"But wait, honey ..." I hung up the phone before Miss Ruby could pry the untapped gossip out of me. My dad really needed her for the interrogation room at the Pecan Bayou Police Department. "Anybody home?" I heard my back door open and shut and the sounds of my son, cousin and aunt all entering.

"I'm in here," I said. Butch barked and scurried across the tile floor in the kitchen, miscalculating where to stop and nearly hitting a wall on the way. As I rounded the corner, Zach screamed in excitement and picked up the slightly damp ball of fur.

"Butch! You came home!" He hugged the little dog so tightly I worried he would break its little bones.

"Um, Zach, if a dog's eyes start to bulge, don't you think you might be hugging him just a little too tight?"

He jumped and then softened his grip. "Oh, Butch, I missed you so much, boy." He looked up at me. "Did he find his way home on his own, or did someone see a poster and bring him to us?" He nestled his nose in Butch's fur. "Oooh, he smells so good!"

I thought about how I should explain this one. Should I tell him I found his little puppy scampering around in the blood of one dead British butler or maybe just tell him about how we're glad he's home? Before I could come up with an answer, Danny blurted it out.

"Somebody went to heaven."

"What do you mean?" Zach asked.

Aunt Maggie put her arm around Zach's shoulders. "Don't you listen to Danny. You have your Butch back, so all's well that ends well."

"But Mama, you told me Butch was there when Mr. Gray's son went to heaven," Danny repeated.

Anxious to get my son off the morbid topic of how many bodies his mother had discovered over the last few years, I went for an easy switch.

"So Danny, how was your day at the vet clinic?"

Danny stopped pulling at his mother's sleeve and smiled his lopsided smile. He pushed up his glasses. "Oh, Allison is wonderful. She works very hard."

"Does she?"

"Yes, we have to mop the floor and then vacuum it too. She does the mop, and I do the vacuuming. We're a good team, she said. I love her."

"Danny," my aunt cautioned, "love is a pretty strong word. Maybe you just like working with her?"

"No, Mama, I love her. We're going to get married."

Aunt Maggie sighed and patted his hand. "What about your other girlfriend? The one from your school?"

"I can't marry both of them, silly." Danny looked at her in shock.

"I didn't say that you would, but don't you think it will hurt her feelings to know that you are saying you love Allison?"

Danny looked down at his Converse high-tops and crossed his arms at his chest. "I love Allison." That was the end of this discussion as far as he was concerned.

Chapter 10

The next morning, Zach and I took Butch over to Dr. Springer's office to make sure he was okay after his days of captivity. Dr. Springer checked him out from head to wiggly tail.

"Now where did you say this dog had been?" Dr. Springer asked as she felt Butch's stomach.

"He was kidnapped," Zach said, not sparing the element of excitement.

"He's a cute little dog. I'm surprised you got him back."

"Mom had to climb over a dead body to get him, but that's never stopped her before."

"Excuse me?"

Okay, that cat was out of the bag. Why did I think of animal metaphors in a vet's office? Curious. "It's a long story."

"You're my only appointment for the next hour. I have time," Dr. Springer said as she examined Butch's paws.

"We found him over at Libby Loper's house." I explained about his crawling under the fence and the eventual finding of the dog next to the dead butler.

"That's quite a tragedy. I'm surprised I haven't seen it in the Pecan Bayou Gazette."

"Don't worry, it'll be there. Rocky at the paper has demanded I stop by after this appointment so he can get an eyewitness interview."

"So you actually found the body of Mr. Grayson. That had to be scary."

"What was really scary was Libby Loper hanging out of the upstairs window. I thought she was going to fall out and kill herself."

"You could have caught her, Mom," Zach said as if I had superhero strength.

"Not likely," I answered.

"So how's she doing now?"

"She was released from the hospital and seems to be coming out of a very long drug-induced fog. I really feel sorry for her. I'm not sure, but I think Hunter Grayson might have been stealing from her. The house was crammed with boxes."

"He was drugging her and then spending her money?"

"Something like that."

"That's awful, poor woman."

"When I ran to get her out of the window, she was on something. You know, I have no idea what she's really like when she's not under the influence, but one thing's for sure – she loved this puppy. I felt bad for having to take him back. With all that was going on I almost wished I could let her keep him."

"Mom!" Zach said.

"I didn't for one minute not plan on returning him to you, Zach, but I think Butch liked her, too. He came to her faster than to me."

"He spent more time with her." Dr. Springer ruffled the fur on Butch's head. "You'd only had the puppy for a day. He might have been the first real friend to come her way in a long while. Do you think she's seeing visitors? I might stop by and tell her how Butch is doing. There are many wonderful dogs up for adoption at the Rescue Me Animal Shelter. Maybe I could take her down there and help her find another little dog."

"That would be really nice."

"Yeah, as long as it's not Butch," Zach added.

"Do you know much about Libby Loper?" I asked.

"Not really. Only what I've seen from walking through the museum down the street," the vet replied.

"Say, would you mind keeping Butch for a few minutes while Zach and I head over to the museum? I think it might help us both in understanding the situation."

"Not a problem. He can visit with Miss Ivy, my bulldog in the back."

We strolled down to the house that had been converted into the Charlie Loper Dead Eye Museum. The structure was a small white house with a short front porch and a black metal Texas historical plaque out front. The door squeaked as we entered, and the smell of musty carpet hit my nose. The inside of the home had been gutted to provide for the many exhibits of movie posters that hung on the wall. In the corner, a life-sized statue of Charlie Loper stood looking at us. The skin of the mannequin was unnaturally pale, and his Stetson was tilted just slightly to the side of his vanilla face. He wore a white shirt with blue stars and rhinestone-filled fringe. Around his neck he sported a red bandanna.

"Cool," Zach said.

The mannequin was holding on to the reins of a full-sized tan horse, whose eyes also seemed to follow us. It was saddled up with Charlie Loper's black floral parade saddle with glittering diamond and half-diamond shapes embedded throughout. For a cowboy, the guy was all about bling.

"Can I help you?" A woman came out from the back room wearing blue jeans, a red western shirt and white nametag that said "Lavonne." Her long grey hair was in a braid that ran down her back.

"Um, we were just down at Dr. Springer's office and stopped in to take a look around."

The woman smiled warmly. "Well, that's mighty kind of you. I'm so sorry you've come at a bad time."

"A bad time?"

"Yes, we've had the most terrible tragedy during the night." She gestured over to a glass case in the opposite corner. Inside the case there was a raised platform covered in black velvet.

"You see, that is where I kept Charlie's guns. Someone broke in and took them during the night. It's the most amazing thing. All of the artifacts are precious, but the diamond saddle is worth tens of thousands of dollars."

"Really?" Zach asked, running over to the case. Having seen his grandfather working a crime scene, he quickly took on his persona, with one hand on his hip and the other stroking his small chin.

"Hmm ... from what I can see, there was no forced entry. The glass has not been shattered."

"That's true," the woman said. "The glass dome over the pistols comes right off. We try to dust around here at least once a day. They still glistened after all these years. Charlie had them specially made."

"So whoever took the pistols just had to lift the dome and take them," I said. "Have you called the police?"

"Oh yes, and the insurance company. It's all so sad. We only have a few things left of Charlie's, and now two more are missing."

"Have you called his daughter, Libby?"

"Libby? I haven't spoken to her in years, but not for lack of trying. She doesn't choose to associate with our little museum. I'm just glad that British fella didn't come over here and see all that we have."

"Why would you feel that way?"

"Oh, just call it instinct, I guess. Once he found out the diamonds on the diamond saddle weren't gemstones, he lost interest. Even with that being said, the way he died was just terrible."

"Yes, I know. That's part of the reason we're here. It's a very long story, but I ended up finding Mr. Grayson."

"Oh, my. That must have been awful for you, dear."

"Yes, it was pretty bad. You might have better luck trying to talk to Libby Loper now. I guess you could say she was being overmedicated."

"Oh, and that foul man was taking advantage of her! No wonder Charlie's ghost has returned. He never could tolerate a villain."

Zach turned around, "Charlie Loper's back? I thought he was dead."

"He has only left us in body, dear. His spirit will always be with us."

"What Lavonne means is Charlie Loper's memory will always be with us," I said. Lavonne winked and nodded her head in agreement.

"How did they get in?"

"Well, we're not totally sure about that. Chief Wilson was over here, and he thinks they might have jimmied the lock?" She said it as if she wasn't sure if she was repeating it right.

I went over to the door and opened it. I hadn't noticed before that there were deep scratches on the doorknob, and the keyhole looked uneven at the top.

"They think someone might have used a screwdriver to break the pins in the lock," Lavonne added. "I have a locksmith coming to replace it later today."

I closed the door and walked over to the pistol case. There were no fingerprints on the glass whatsoever.

"It looks so clean. Did the police dust for prints?"

"Well, thank you for that. I use my own special mixture to keep the glass sparkling. I'd like to think Charlie would have wanted it that way. Whoever took the guns must have worn gloves, because the police didn't pick up anything."

"I write the Happy Hinter column for the newspaper, and I'd love to get your recipe for glass cleaner," I said.

"You do? You know, I thought I recognized you from the moment you came in. Why, I'd just be honored to have my recipe in the paper. Let me just go in the back and write it down for you."

She turned around in the quiet room full of artifacts and then spread her arm across the area. "Please feel free to take a look around and enjoy the museum." She exited through some cow-print curtains, and Zach and I resumed our wandering.

"Mom, look at this," he said, walking over to an alcove roped off with fence posts and twine. "This must have been Charlie Loper's bedroom." They had recreated what looked like a bedroom set from the '30s, and around the bed were many pictures and movie posters of Charlie Loper. There was another copy of the picture of Libby Loper on a white horse and an old rocking chair. Next to the bed was a glass case with small personal items like pocket knives and antique shaving kits.

"Here we go." Lavonne returned from the back room waving a 3x5 index card. "Oh, this is so exciting. Could you make sure you say something about the museum when you write the article? Business has been a little slow, and donations are down."

"I think as long as we have the Pecan Bayou Gazette resurrecting Charlie, you'll get plenty of visitors," I replied.

Chapter 11

"So let me get this straight – you climbed over the fence to get this little fella?" Rocky leaned back in his chair and chuckled. This was the biggest story that had hit the paper since Zelda Sue Stevens thought her pecan tree was waving to her. His grizzled face could have been that of a cowboy who had endured years of soul-draining dust on the trail. What Rocky had endured was years of slow news in a small town. Even with that, he had a gift for making even the most mundane bake sale into a true excitement. He chewed on his yellow Dixon Ticonderoga pencil and then added a few things to an overfilled yellow legal pad. He leaned forward in a confidential matter and asked, "Just how angry were you with this man for stealing your dog and then lying about it?"

I gasped and then had to laugh at his hard-boiled reporter approach. "Not angry enough to kill him."

"So you admit a prior relationship with him."

"If you count yelling at him through an intercom, then yes, we were involved."

The front door to the quiet office opened, letting in a rush of heat from the street.

"Mr. Whitson?" A woman stood on the other side of the classified ad counter. Rocky rose from his squeaking ancient office chair and strode over, his cowboy boots clicking against the linoleum. I could see a small girl standing next to her, playing a handheld video game.

"Can I help you, ma'am?" Rocky smiled and took out a pad of forms for classifieds.

"You certainly can. I was wondering if there was going to be a photo layout of the contestants in the Miss Watermelon Pageant?" Oh God, another pageant mom. Carrying the requisite oversized handbag, she pulled out a slim leather binder and opened it on the counter. "As you can see, we have a full portfolio of Tiffy here. Would you rather have her formal attire or her jazzy casual look?"

Rocky took in a deep breath and smiled. "Quite impressive, ma'am. You've really done your homework ..."

"I thank you. I feel my job is to manage my daughter's pageant experience in a positive yet productive way ..."

"... but we aren't doing any special layouts of the contestants. We will be featuring a picture of the winner once she's crowned."

The woman's eyebrows raised in astonishment. "Really?" Her tone dropped ever so slightly at the end. This was not what mama wanted to hear.

"Yes, ma'am. The Miss Watermelon Pageant the paper is sponsoring is really more for fun than anything else. But of course, as you just put it so well, you want your daughter's experience to be positive. Putting all the little girls' pictures in the paper might make it too competitive, don't you think?"

"I think that is precisely what needs to be done. How can the community possibly have enough time to evaluate our little darlings if they can't look at their photos at their leisure?"

"The community, as you put it, is not going to be judging the contest. The paper is." The phone on Rocky's desk rang, and he stepped back toward me. I wondered if I could possibly slip out the back door before the woman noticed I was there. "In fact, we have one of the judges right here." He motioned toward me as he picked up the phone to answer it. I had been holding Butch in case he decided to leave a puddle on the floor, but now he squirmed out of my arms to the tile. I flashed a lopsided smile and waved. Zach ran after Butch, and the little girl put away her toy and started through the classified counter gate to pet the puppy.

The woman, whose face had formerly been a mixture of rage and dissatisfaction with the paper's lack of publicity now turned on me. "Well, what a pleasure to get to meet you before the pageant Miss ... Miss?"

I think she expected me to use my pageant name, like "the former Miss Bluebonnet," which I guess is a whole lot better than a stripper name. Alas, I had never trod the runway, so I would just have to introduce myself as "the Happy Hinter."

"Hi, I'm Betsy Livingston. I write the Happy Hinter column for the newspaper." The lady extended her hand with the overly heavy handbag strap weighing down her arm. She took her other hand and grabbed her daughter by the scruff of the neck, pulling her away from Zach and the puppy.

"Tiffy, this nice lady is going to be your judge. What do you have to say to her?"

"Um, nice to meet you." She shyly put out her hand, and I shook it. "What's your puppy's name?"

"This is Butch," Zach said. "He was dog-napped."

"Dog-napped? Wow." She was in absolute awe.

"Miss Livingston, let me leave you some of Tiffy's portfolio. You will find some wonderful shots of her in here."

"No, no. I couldn't," I answered.

"But you must," she insisted.

"No, really, it wouldn't be fair to have your daughter's pictures and none of the other girls' pictures. Let's just save it all for pageant day, okay?"

She slapped the deep brown portfolio closed. "Of course." She grabbed her daughter back from the puppy once again. "Tiffy, let's go."

"Aw mom, I was playing with the puppy."

"We'll be late for your dance class. Let's go."

Tiffy looked forlorn and slowly waved goodbye to Zach.

"Bye, Tiffy," Zach said.

Rocky hung up the phone and reached for his cowboy hat. "Betsy, we're going to have to reschedule. Got a story I need to go out on." He grabbed his keys from his desk drawer.

"Sure, what's the story?"

Rocky headed to the front of the office and flipped the lights and turned the "Open" sign to "Back Soon." "Don't know all the details yet. Have to tell you about it later." We followed him out the door into the heat, quite similar to opening the oven door on Thanksgiving.

Chapter 12

Deciding to celebrate Butch's arrival back home, Zach and I picked up some hamburgers and headed for the town park. The park, which served as a town meeting place with a gazebo on one side and Lake Pecan on the other, had recently bought the land where the old Dairy Queen had stood and sectioned it off for a dog park. There were two sections, one side for big dogs and the other side for small dogs. There were several park benches under the pecan trees and a water fountain designed just for dogs squirting water at both low and high levels. Most of the time dogs didn't mess with each other too much at the park. They were happy if someone, anyone, would just throw a ball. Butch went scrambling across the well-fertilized grass, his puppy paws clumsily padding the ground. I was surprised to see Sunshine the beagle taking a slurp of water. Standing next to her was the same man I had met outside Dr. Springer's office. Upon seeing us he waved and walked over.

"I see you found your puppy. That's great," he said. Today he was dressed in maroon and navy plaid shorts and a T-shirt that revealed he'd visited the gym about a hundred times more than me this year.

"Yes, we did." Should I explain the grisly circumstances of my rescue or spare this guy who was so new to town? Probably not a great commercial for the Chamber of Commerce to reveal to him that murder was alive and well in Pecan Bayou.

"He looks like he fared pretty well on his journey." He looked down at his watch. "I really didn't have time to do this, but Sunshine is having a hard time adjusting to the new house. My yard is fenced, but if there's a hole anywhere she'll snoop it out and squeeze through it. She found one, so here we are." He picked up a suit jacket he had placed across a bench in the shade. "Nice to see you again, but I really have to be getting back to my office." He pulled a leash out of his pocket, but stopped mid-stride and turned toward me. "Would it be too much for me to ask you if you would be interested in having dinner with me? I hear there's a great restaurant on the bayou."

This was a surprise. A nice, attractive guy asking me out while I perspired in the heat and brushed puppy paw dirt off my shorts. Had all the other single women in town moved away? I considered him for a moment and then the face of a stormy weatherman flashed through my brain.

"We could bring along your son as well. I just didn't want to eat alone," he added.

My lips formed a line. "Thank you for your invitation, but I think I need to pass. By the way, you're right. Ben's Bayou Restaurant is wonderful. I highly recommend the steak covered in onion sauce. It's really good."

He stepped back and bowed his head slightly. "I'll have to order that, then." He whistled for his dog, who came running over. Clipping his leash onto her collar, he started walking back to the gate. "Glad you got your dog back."

I sat in the shaded area and unwrapped my cheeseburger. I set Zach's bag of food on the bench, deciding to let him play just a little longer. I had been dating Leo Fitzpatrick for almost two years now, and the thought of being asked out by someone else just wasn't on my radar. Leo lived in Dallas and worked as a meteorologist for the weather service there. He was raising his sister's son after her untimely death, and even though our relationship was long-distance, it seemed to be working for now. The man with the beagle was handsome, well-dressed and looked successful, but you could have said that about my first husband. My phone rang in my purse, and I reached over for it.

"Betsy? Where are you?" My dad asked.

"We're over at the dog park with Butch. Rocky had to cancel his interview for some big news story. Know anything about that?"

"Uh, no. I don't know what he's up to. Probably a big stink over at the diner when they ran out of peanut butter pie. I packed my lunch today, so I'll head on over. I got somethin' I want to talk to you about."

Within ten minutes, my dad pulled up in his squad car and stepped through the squeaky gate of the chain link fence. "Hey Butch, how ya doing there, fella?" Butch ran up to him in full-tilt crazy mode.

"He'll love you even more for part of your sandwich." My dad straightened up in his blue uniform, a little thin for a man in his fifties, but that probably had something to do with how hard he worked. A faint whiff of Old Spice drifted over.

He settled down on the park bench next to me as Zach, grown tired of playing, now slurped on his milkshake. Pulling a ham sandwich out of a baggie, he motioned to Zach. "Say, Zach, why don't you go play with Butch for a minute while I talk to your mother."

"It's hot out there." Zach's cheeks were red from his exertion. Butch had settled down next to him, panting so hard his tongue looked like it would fall out of his mouth.

"Just give me a minute. Why don't you go squirt Butch with the hose?" There was a "dog washing" area with a garden hose hooked up over at the former drive-through area of the Dairy Queen.

"Okay." With the idea of having permission to play in the water, Zach shot off the bench.

My dad swiped at some sweat on his nose. "Artie at the coroner's office says it was blunt-force trauma. Somebody beaned him on the head pretty good."

"Do you have any idea who might have done it?"

"Not yet, and the murder weapon is definitely that concrete pedestal you found in the bushes. There were pieces of Grayson's brain on it."

"So what are you going to do?"

"It's more like what you're going to do."

I wadded up my wax-coated burger wrapper. "I don't work for the police, did you forget?"

"Libby Loper is a prime suspect because of the fact that Grayson was stealing her blind. We've questioned her some, but I think she might be hiding something. A few harmless questions couldn't hurt. I'd like you to go over and offer to help clean and reorganize her house – and in the process if you come across something, then leave it there in an obvious place," he said. "It is part of what you do, after all. You write organizational tips in the paper all the time. Well, here's your chance to use some of them. What do you say?"

"I say it's crazy. What if she figures out what I'm up to?"

"If we are going to issue a search warrant anyway, what's the difference? Your efforts will help the rest of us to actually find something before Christmas."

"Okay," I consented.

"Now that's the cowboy way, darlin'."

Chapter 13

The next morning as I ate my cereal and watched the sun shine through the kitchen windows, I unfolded the latest edition of the Pecan Bayou Gazette. Looking for my pictures of the Bonnet Farm, I didn't have to search too long. My picture of the shed was front and center, but not with the headline "Watermelons Bountiful at Bonnet Farm." Instead it said, "Lt. Judd Kelsey Accused of Planting Evidence." The picture I had taken of the outbuildings showed the many tourists visiting the farm that day. My little Miss Watermelon hopeful and her mother were there, and my father was bent over, looking like he was placing something on the ground near Coop Bonnet's red Corvette. I couldn't believe Rocky put this in without telling me about it first. I read the article below the photo.

Judd Kelsey was accused by Clay Bonnet of planting drug paraphernalia in the car of his son, Coop Bonnet, leading him to be arrested for possession on Tuesday. The new district attorney, Adam Cole, is pursuing an investigation of Officer Kelsey, who has been put on limited duty until the issue is resolved.

"I was sure he was planting something on my son's car, and then he comes up with a bag of pot," said Clay Bonnet. "This is police harassment, and we will fight it all the way up to the Supreme Court if need be."

Inset into my own picture was a picture of a familiar face. This was the guy with the beagle. His handsome smile and kind face looked so trustworthy. Not the first time I had been duped by that sort of thing. He was the new district attorney investigating my dad?

I grabbed for the phone, unsure who to call first – Dad or Rocky. I started to dial Rocky's number when my phone rang in my hand, almost scaring me to death.

"Betsy. Have you read the paper?" Aunt Maggie asked on the other end of the line.

"I just saw it."

"Did you take that picture?"

"Yes, I did, but I had no idea it would lead to Dad being investigated. I was just about to call Rocky and ask him why he didn't warn me he changed the story."

"Rocky can't help himself when he sniffs out a story. You have to realize that."

"Even when the story involves a friend?"

"Especially if it involves a friend. He would see it as an opportunity for more access to news."

"I get your point. Rocky is Pecan Bayou's one and only paparazzi."

"I've never heard your dad talk about this district attorney, so I don't even know how serious all of this is. I do know my brother would never plant evidence."

"I've met the district attorney," I said quietly.

"You're in league with both the newspaper and the devil, – I mean, the DA?"

"No, I'm not in league with anyone. I met him outside Dr. Springer's office. He was very kind when we told him about losing Butch. Then I met him again at the dog park."

"You met him at the dog park? Do you mean you happened to see him there or you 'met' him?"

"No, I didn't meet him that way. I just ran into him, that's all. He asked me out on a date."

"But you're not in cahoots with him in any way?" Maggie said slowly as if trying to understand why I seemed to be involved with every part of my father's crisis.

"No, Aunt Maggie, I'm not. Why would I ever do anything to harm my father?"

"You're right, I know. I just wish I could find out more about this guy. He could be just going along with Clay Bonnet to humor him or maybe he really believes him. It might be a way to clean out what he thinks might be a corrupt small-town police force. Have you talked to your father?" Maggie asked.

"I was just about to call him when you rang through," I said.

"Well, don't. He's in a meeting with Chief Wilson. I called him, and he said for me to be calm and we would discuss it as a family later."

A family meeting. Who were we, the Brady Bunch? My dad had to be pretty upset about this. He could end up losing his job because of my picture. It really was my fault, and of course that would be the one Rocky would choose for the front page of the paper. Like Maggie, I just wish I knew if Adam Cole would seriously pursue this. Maybe I could call him? I could probably get his number from the city offices directory, or even Dr. Springer could help. A thought occurred to me. Maybe I could do even more than that.

"Aunt Maggie, what would you say if I accepted that date with Adam Cole?"

"Oh, honey, I don't think your womanly wiles could change his mind."

"No, that's not what I mean. So far, he doesn't seem to know I'm the daughter of his cop under investigation. I could just casually talk to him about his work and find out what he thinks of the case."

"What about Leo?"

"What *about* Leo?" I countered. "Even though Adam Cole is a very handsome man, I'm not dating him for real. I'm going undercover."

"Don't put it that way."

"You know what I mean."

"Well," Maggie paused for a moment as she thought about it. "I guess it couldn't hurt." She was quiet again. "I don't think you should tell your father about this. He'd shut you down quicker than a fireworks stand in a drought."

"Snap, crackle, pop."

Chapter 14

Trying to find Adam Cole wouldn't be too difficult. I already knew he was taking Sunshine to the dog park every day at noon. Zach, Butch and I packed a picnic lunch and headed back over to accidentally-on-purpose run into Mr. Cole. Zach of course, had no idea the sneaky thing his mother was about to do. He was more than a little curious as to why I wanted to go to the dog park when it looked like it was going to rain. At the last minute I threw an umbrella into our bag. Right as we entered the dog park, the sky burst open and a healthy Texas downpour drenched us.

"Mom, it's raining. Let's go back home," Zach said as I scrambled to open the umbrella. We couldn't go back home. What if this was my only chance to come in contact with Adam Cole and save my dad's reputation?

"Come on, Zach. Butch doesn't mind if it's raining, now do you, Butch?" Butch looked up at me, his little tail between his legs, the water starting to make him look like a large rodent just crawling out of the sewer.

I clutched my picnic basket and headed for the covered benches and tables. The lightning crackled just as we got to the shelter.

"Mom, is this a metal roof? Is that safe in a thunderstorm?"

I tried to ignore my son and the intelligence he was producing from that darned public school education.

"We'll be fine." I pulled out our peanut butter sandwiches and tried to make light of the situation. Butch now cowered under the picnic table.

"Mom, are you crazy? We need to get out of here," Zach pleaded. I was just about to take him up on it when I heard a voice from behind me.

"Betsy?" It was Adam Cole, holding his briefcase over his head and dragging along Sunshine, who was, needless to say, not feeling her name.

"Hi there," I chirped. "What a surprise to see you here!"

"I could say the same. You must really love that little dog to bring him out in the rain like this."

"Yes, we really love him ... Uh, and it wasn't raining when we got here," I assured him. I ran a hand through my hair, sure the humidity was turning it into a layer of frizz. "So you didn't get your fence fixed yet?" I asked.

"No, I've been pretty busy at work. New job, you know."

"Yes, new job, new town." I put on my most seductive smile and then took a little too big of a bite of my sandwich.

"Boy, you must be hungry," he said, noticing the hunk I had just taken out of my sandwich. That was it! That was my path to getting him to talk about dinner. I tried to answer him, but found the peanut butter wasn't budging. I muttered incomprehensibly, but he stopped me.

"Take your time, you'll choke." He reached over and patted me on the back like I was a four-year-old who had gobbled down too much cookie.

I finally swallowed and took a breath of air. "Yes, I was hungry." Zach was now looking at me closely, probably wondering if he needed to arrange a nursing home for his loony mother.

Adam Cole turned back toward his dog and tried to push her out into the rain beyond the somewhat dry space we were in. She wasn't having it.

"I was just saying," I said too loudly. He jumped and turned around from the dog. "I was just saying to a friend of mine that it's really nice to eat with someone who's over eighteen sometimes."

A look of confusion came over Zach's face.

Cole smiled. "You don't get to do that?"

"Well, you know," I motioned to Zach. "Being a single parent, I don't get to converse with adults all that much."

"Oh," he nodded. I was sure he was going to launch into the dinner invite one more time, but a quiet settled between us as the rhythm of the falling rain pounded on the tin roof above us. This was not happening. My Mata Hari was truly inadequate.

"I'll go to dinner," I blurted out.

"Oh, um ... great," he said. "I didn't think you wanted to go to dinner. I thought you might have a boyfriend or something."

"She does," Zach interrupted.

"Well, we're just going to dinner, Zach. That's all. No harm in that."

Zach folded his arms over and turned away from me. Butch scooted to the other side of the concrete.

Nobody ever said the spy game was easy.

*****

Feeling more than a twinge of guilt for setting up a date with another man, I made a call to Leo. He came into my life after a long dry spell of waiting for a husband who disappeared. Fearing that he had been the victim of foul play, I raised our son by myself but never quite let go of hoping he would return. When he finally did come back into my life, I confirmed the suspicions I had feared all along. He was nothing more than a con man who had moved on to other lives and other women.

Thank goodness that when the truth was finally revealed to me, I was already involved with Leo. Through all of my mishaps, Leo seemed to be supportive and understanding. A guy like that doesn't come along every day, but to be truthful I wasn't totally sure how I felt about him. He lived in another city, so our time together had been scattered. Still, although I found myself wishing he were around more than just a weekend here and weekend there, if we lived in the same city together would the chemistry be the same, seeing each other day after day? Could I deal with having a father for Zach when I had been doing the job for so many years? There was so much unknown about our future that I felt the anxiety creeping in, coupled with an overwhelming feeling of fear that I could lose this wonderful man.

I punched in the Dallas number. It was still early in the hurricane season, so he shouldn't be too overtaken by work yet. When Leo talked about the tropics, he wasn't eying the beaches thinking of relaxation and a margarita. He was eying those swirling clouds that formed off of Africa and then calculating if they were heading for the Gulf. What a romantic. What he lacked in beach etiquette he made up for in everything else. He was for sure the one guy I wouldn't mind being stranded on a deserted island with. Well, maybe him and air conditioning and that margarita, I thought as I felt the heat of July beating through my kitchen window.

"Hello?"

"Hey, it's Betsy."

"Hi there. Nice to hear your voice on this overcast summer day."

"Yours too. We found Zach's dog."

"Oh, that's great. Tyler's been bugging me to come down there to meet him. Now I guess we have a reason."

"You didn't need the dog to come down."

Leo chuckled. "Nice to know."

"He was kidnapped by the people whose fence he ran under. They just kept him. I would never have known, but I went back to the locked gate, and there he was running around in their courtyard." I took a breath before I added the last part, "And I, uh, found a body."

It was quiet on the other end. This was the third time this had happened, and I was trying to gauge his response. From the silence that followed, I would have to predict an oncoming storm.

"Leo?"

"Betsy? What is the crime rate in that town? My God, was there some sort of aerial crop spraying that got out of hand or something and turned half the brains of the residents to mush?"

"No," I answered. "At least I don't think so." I continued to tell him the story of the dead butler and Libby Loper.

"So you climbed over the fence?"

"Yes, I did. Aunt Maggie helped."

"Your partner in crime."

"She'd like hearing that," I replied. "Well, I just wanted to let you know I was thinking of you and that we found Butch."

"Now that I know your latest adventure, I'll be thinking and mostly worrying about you," he said. "I might be able to get away a little earlier than the fourth with Tyler. It's so hard to keep an eye on you when we're three hours apart."

I thought about the dinner plans I had just made with Adam Cole. If Leo showed up, it would be pretty hard to explain why I was "dating" the new guy in town. It would be better to keep him in Dallas until the fourth.

"No, we're fine. Honest. You need to work and not be running down here every time I ... every time I ..."

"Find a body?"

"Well, yes."

"Okay, we'll be in then on Saturday morning for the big day. Can't wait to see you."

"Me too," I said, a slight quiver in my voice.

"Stay safe," he added.

"Of course."

Chapter 15

The next day, after a short phone call to Libby Loper, I reported for duty to help clean up the mess Hunter Grayson had made of her house. I thought she would balk at the thought of some stranger wanting to come in, but she welcomed the help, especially when I enlisted Maggie to come along.

Maggie opened a tattered cardboard box. "Now what in the world would a man need with all of these vases? Was he going to be openin' a flower shop?"

"I have no idea. The general plan is, make a stack of items for Libby to look through, and what she doesn't want we either try to return or sell." I had set up three areas to organize the items – one to throw away, one to donate and one to keep.

"Some of this stuff looks like it has been here for years. I don't think they'll be lettin' you return it."

I dusted off an unopened box and opened it with a carpet knife. Through a blanket of Styrofoam peanuts, I pulled up another vase. "Another vase. I'll put it in the donation pile."

"Again I say, who needs all these vases? Been to the Goodwill store? The clothes get bought, and the vases get dusty," said Maggie.

"Just be sure to keep all the paperwork with each item," Libby Loper said as she leaned into the door with a cup of coffee. Now sober, she looked like a completely different person. Her stringy hair was now cut, curled and sprayed thanks to the wonders of Miss Ruby at the Hair House. She wore a green silk blouse over white slacks, and her wrists clinked with coordinating bracelets. If I had to guess the stores she bought that outfit in, I would have to say Nordstrom's or Neiman Marcus.

"Yes, Ma'am, we've been putting the invoices inside the vases."

"Do you have any idea how much Hunter Grayson spent here?" I asked.

Libby shook her head. "He went on the Internet and ordered something every day for two years. I've just retained a new attorney to rewrite my will. Whoever this Irving Spalding guy was, he was hired by Hunter. He didn't seem to be too worried that my signature was obtained while I was under the influence of sedatives."

"Amazin', isn't it?" Aunt Maggie said.

"I'm just sorry he's dead." Maggie and I exchanged glances as Libby continued. "I would have liked to cart that man off to jail."

The doorbell on the first floor rang. Libby smiled and said, "I guess I'd better get used to getting the door myself for a while. You ladies are doing a wonderful job." She ran her hand over a cardboard box and left the room. I counted two diamond rings and a diamond watch just on that hand. It wouldn't be too long before she had "help."

I stretched my aching back and looked around at the boxes we still had to open in this room. It was surprising he could get this much stuff in here. I bet the UPS guy could give us more details about Hunter Grayson than anyone else in the entire town. Grayson was probably his kid's godfather they had to be spending so much time together. Libby returned to the packed room holding a white casserole dish covered in foil. Behind her stood the vet, Dr. Springer.

"Surprise, Dr. Springer brought us some lunch," she said cheerfully. The aroma from the casserole started drifting over, and the idea of lunch seemed pretty good. Behind Libby walked both Jean Springer and her intern, Allison.

"This is our day off from the clinic. We thought we might come over and help, if that's okay."

"Okay? I think it's a great idea. More hands make less work," said Maggie as she handed Allison a carpet knife. "You can start opening those boxes over there, dear."

"Wow, this certainly is a lot of stuff," Dr. Springer said, stating the obvious.

"Yes. Betsy is an efficiency expert, and she graciously volunteered to help me straighten it up," Libby said.

"I had no idea." Jean Springer turned to me and placed her hand on my sleeve. "How is Butch?"

Libby's eyes registered something that could have been jealousy. I wasn't sure. It had to be painful hearing about him – after all, he was her dog for a week, even if she had been traipsing in and out of reality.

"He's fine. Glad to be home." I stopped there, not wanting to hurt Libby.

"It was unfortunate that he came to me the way he did," Libby said quietly.

"I know it must have been tough giving him up, but one of the reasons I came by was to tell you about all of the pets we have available for adoption. Butch was a rescue dog, and we would love to help you find another."

Libby smiled. "No, I'm a little old to be wanting a puppy, don't you think?"

"You're never too old for a puppy," Aunt Maggie said.

"Maybe so," Libby said, hugging the warm casserole dish. "We all know the man thing didn't work for me, so maybe a dog?"

"At least they're loyal," Dr. Springer said, patting her shoulder. She would have to use the word loyal, making me remember my guilt over seeing Adam Cole for dinner. I realized that if I hadn't been trying to help my dad, I never would have considered going out with Adam. I blew the dust off of a cut-glass serving dish.

"After we finish in here, we'll start cleaning out Mr. Grayson's closet."

"That will be a fine haul for Goodwill. Hunter only wore the finest cashmere, linen and wool. Even his pajamas were pure silk," Libby Loper said. Just how much he had done for her? Had there been more than a butler/lady of the house relationship?

"Ladies, each one of you grab an empty box and put all you want in it," Libby said. "Saves me the time and trouble of getting rid of some of this junk."

Maggie picked up a box and handed it to me. "Here, Betsy. You take this one, and I'll grab the one over there. We ought to find some real nice stuff here. Thanks, Libby."

"My pleasure," Libby returned. Dr. Springer and Allison each picked up their empty boxes.

"What's this I hear about Judd being in some sort of trouble?" Dr. Springer asked me. "Your father has always been so kind. He brings us strays sometimes before animal control gets to them. He knows we can find homes for them through our rescue operation. I was shocked to see his picture in the paper."

I paused, not sure how much he would want me to share about the situation.

Maggie spoke up before I could. "He didn't do it. Clay Bonnet accused him of planting evidence on that wild boy of his. As if anything needed to be planted with that kid."

Allison nodded and sliced open a box. She started pulling out what looked like a purple velvet shower curtain.

Aunt Maggie went over and felt the fabric. "Oh my, I think I might have to put that in my box. This is just beautiful."

"Well, I think it's terrible, about Lieutenant Kelsey, I mean," said Libby Loper. "How did they ever get a picture like that? Someone had to be there at the farm that day to get it and then turn it into the newspaper. Who would do that?"

"I did it," I replied meekly.

The room went quiet as the ladies tried to figure how to politely get themselves out of this awkward situation.

"Let me explain," I said. "I took the picture for a series of articles we are doing for the upcoming Watermelon Festival. My dad just happened to be in the picture, and Rocky used it."

"So," Aunt Maggie said as she slit open a box. "Judd could of been picking flowers for all we know, but Rocky Whitless decides to put it in the paper as planting evidence."

"That's terrible," Dr. Springer said, fingering her glasses that hung on a pink-and-green beaded chain.

"You have grounds to sue him, you know," Allison added.

"We could, but Rocky is an old friend," I said.

"Old friend or not, he could have just ended your father's career."

"No, my dad is innocent, and hopefully the district attorney will see that."

"Clay Bonnet is nothing but trash," Maggie said. "I wish you'd gotten a picture of his son Coop lightin' one up. That would have stopped all this." The ladies laughed as my aunt imitated someone smoking a joint.

"Aunt Maggie, stop that," I said over the noise, holding back a giggle.

Libby looked around the room. "I can't tell you how much you are doing for me, organizing all of this. I really look forward to the day I can enjoy my home again. I just had no idea he was stockpiling all this."

"Can I take this down and put it in your kitchen?" asked Dr. Springer, reaching for the casserole dish.

"Oh, yes. I'm sorry. It smells delicious. Why don't we have a little break then and all enjoy some of the casserole?" Libby said.

"I'd love a piece," my aunt said, inviting herself. "How about you, Betsy?"

"No, I think I'll work just a little longer. I may have to leave early to get Zach."

"Suit yourself. Allison?"

"No, thank you. I had a big breakfast," Allison said, pulling tiny glass figurines out of a box. The other three ladies left us alone to dig through the dusty mess. I opened a desk drawer and pulled out a large journal. It had blue and gold flowers on the cover and seemed to be filled with poetry. Bad poetry.

"What did you find?"

"Oh, it seems Hunter liked to write poetry," I said. Allison laughed.

"Ugh, please don't read any of it to me," she said. "I had enough of that in boarding school."

"I'll bet it didn't sound like this." I began reading, "In the glen there is a secret, one I cannot, will not tell. In the glen there is a secret, for the ones who cannot see."

"That's ... really bad. Who was he writing that stuff for, anyway?"

"Who knows. I need to take it to my dad. This is the kind of thing he will look at and figure out." I stuck the floral notebook in my box.

"Your dad is going to interpret poetry and solve the case?" she asked.

"Sure, what cop doesn't enjoy a little iambic pentameter?" I countered. "I just hope I can remember to take it out of my car. Maggie will be glad to tell you that I have the messiest car in the family. I tend to get distracted and forget to bring the groceries in sometimes."

I searched through the rest of the desk stuffed with receipts and bills, which I started stacking in piles. Allison started breaking down some of the boxes and folding them in the corner. I knew this would be a good time to talk about Danny.

"Allison, Danny just loves working with you."

"And I love working with him," she answered.

"Yes, well sometimes, when he's around somebody who is young and pretty and ..."

"I get it. He has a crush on me?"

I felt relief flooding through me. "Yes! He has told me how wonderful you are."

"He's told me that, too."

"Will you let him down easy?" I asked.

"Yes, I'll tell him I have a boyfriend. That ought to help."

"If you do, just promise you'll do it very gently."

"Of course," she said and then hugged my shoulder. Danny was in good hands.

Chapter 16

As soon as I was able to get away from Libby Loper's house, I poked my head into the Pecan Bayou Police Department. I found my dad behind his desk, busily hunting and pecking the keys on his keyboard. His typing skills were questionable, but dependable.

Upon seeing me, he leaned back in his chair to address Mrs. Thatcher, engrossed in a puzzle book at the dispatcher's desk. "Betsy's here. I think I'll be taking my coffee break now."

"Whatever," she said, barely looking up. "I'll let you know if a crime wave up and hits us."

"Thank you, ma'am," he said. He stepped out from behind the counter and took me by the arm. "What do you say we check out Earl's?"

We walked three doors down to Earl's Java. The bell tinkled as we walked in. Earl was leaning back in a brown leather booth, snoring softly. Hot coffee on a summer afternoon in Texas wasn't too much of a moneymaker. My father picked up the coffee pot and a cup and helped himself.

"Shouldn't we wake up Earl?"

"Nah, I just leave money on the counter. It's a system."

"If you say so." I walked over and grabbed a soft drink from the cooler. We climbed into the cool leather booth on the other side of the restaurant as a fan gently hummed above us.

"So, what did you find?" my father asked.

"Not much. A whole lot of glassware and a book of poetry so far. I have it out in the car if you'd like to see it."

My father shot a glance at the sleeping Earl. "Poetry? Really?"

"It might give you some insight into the victim."

He considered it for a moment and then nodded his head. "Okay, bring it to me and I'll check it out. You didn't find anything else like maybe the guns that were stolen from the museum?"

"No, and I looked everywhere."

"If you find the gun, then you have the killer. Easy as that – and if Libby has those guns, then she's the ..." Earl stirred in the corner, silencing my dad.

"I just wish you could do more, Dad." I whispered. "Libby looks like a lost sheep in that house. Imagine waking up to find out someone else has been living in your house, drugging you and having a shopping spree with your savings."

"Do you think Grayson cleaned her out?"

"Hard to tell. She's packing some bling, that's for sure. Aunt Maggie says she's making an income off of her father's estate. Someone made a heck of a deal all those years ago. Now that his old movies are on DVD, she is probably making a pretty good income off them."

"Well, at least that's good to know about her. She doesn't have much recourse against Grayson except to try to sell or return the stuff he was stockpiling."

"There is no way on earth he could have ever used or even displayed all that junk. You never know if the thrill was owning it or just being able to buy it. It's shopper's high."

"Unfortunately the bill always comes due, right?"

"Right." My thoughts drifted to the investigation my dad was going through from the Bonnet arrest. Was that a bill that was due? He had always been there for me. Not only was I not able to help, I was the one who helped frame him. Sitting there, watching him sip at his coffee, I wondered what he would think of my trying to get information out of Adam Cole. Better to do it and ask permission later.

After I returned home, I pulled up the pictures I had taken at the Bonnet Farm. Maybe, just maybe I could find something that would help out my dad. The first shot I pulled up was the one of my father "planting evidence." He really did look like he was just picking something up. It could also be interpreted the wrong way, especially if you had a guilty son you wanted to look innocent.

Dad was standing up against the shed. I enlarged the picture to see what was in there. Coop Bonnet talking on his cell phone leaning up against the shed. He didn't look too guilty of anything unless it was taking a personal call on his father's time. I looked through the rest of the pictures. I had taken several of the rows of watermelons skirting up against a wooded area. Those were the pictures I thought Rocky would use, not one accusing my father of planting evidence. I had tried to get a picture of the house from the field of watermelons, but they didn't seem to want me over there. I needed to go back and see the farm again, but after what happened the last time I didn't see Clay Bonnet being too friendly with me. Maybe if I could take Zach and say I was there having a teaching moment kind of visit they would put up with me. Just one more look around might help me turn up something.

Chapter 17

"Mom! How big of a watermelon can we buy?" Zach said, holding Butch by his leash. The little dog was squirming to run as he viewed puppy heaven. Miles and miles of to nothing to do but run.

"Yeah, how big, Betsy?" Danny echoed.

"Um, let's get a big one," I answered.

Zach and Danny let out a whoop and started running up and down the rows of watermelons. Butch, coming from behind, now led the way, dragging them along behind him. I followed them but made a wide turn, making my way back to the trees. I wanted to step back and look at the farm from a different angle.

"Betsy?" I heard Lina Bonnet's voice from behind me.

"Hi, Lina," I said a little too cheerily.

"I'm surprised to see you here."

"Oh, well," I said, flapping my hands to the side, "the boys just had to get a watermelon for the Fourth, you know."

"Oh," she said, fingering a gold pendant at her neck that was circled in what looked like emeralds. It was a pretty nice necklace for a farm girl. The sun caught the stones, creating a blinding effect back at me. "Well, there are some beauties up toward the house."

I turned toward the boys, and they were running closer and closer to the trees. It seemed that Butch had wriggled out of his collar again and was making a beeline toward the woods.

"Oh no, excuse me, we have to get the dog," I said to Lina.

"I'll help." She ran to the other row, trying to corner the puppy. All four of us closed in on him, and I noticed that Clay Bonnet was now out in the field helping to capture Butch.

"Here, boy," Clay whistled. I wasn't so sure I wanted Butch to actually come to him. We all converged on him right as Zach reached down to swoop him up. Butch, having none of this, wriggled free and hightailed it back to the woods. He was closest to me, so I ran after him to the edge of the elm and pecan trees. I was about two feet in when Clay, with amazing agility, came up through the trees from the other side and grabbed Butch. I stood on the edge of the tree line breathing hard. I used the opportunity to see further into the woods. A hammock hung between two of the trees, and there was trash strewn about in the weeds on the ground under it. It looked like a nice cool place for field workers to take a little break and then leave trash.

"Thank you so much, Mr. Bonnet," I said, my hands on my knees as I gasped for breath.

Clay Bonnet handed me the wriggling Butch and, grabbing my elbow, guided me back out. "You really shouldn't be bringing a dog out here, Mrs. Livingston. They could get you into all sorts of trouble," he said under his breath.

"Yeah, thanks, Mr. Bonnet," Danny said, pronouncing Clay Bonnet's name like the hat a prairie girl would wear.

"You need to keep this dog on his leash," he said as I handed the dog back to Zach, who started trying to put Butch's collar back on.

"Yes, he keeps getting free," I said. "It would have been awful if he had gotten into some of the trash around the hammock." I guess I had just seen the underbelly of the farm. It was quite a contrast to the pristine blue-and-white painted farmhouse gleaming in the hot July sun.

Anxious to lighten the mood, I plunged in as if we hadn't just been rounded up by the people who were threatening to get my dad relieved of duty. "Did you guys find a watermelon?" I asked the boys.

Danny and Zach sprinted two rows over as they both settled on a watermelon the size of a small wagon. "This one! This one! Can we pick it?" Zach shouted.

"Sure," I said.

Clay Bonnet took off his baseball cap and swatted at a bug around his head. His lips tightened into a line. As we came upon the produce stand the Bonnet farm used to ring up sales, Clay gestured to Lina.

"You can pay Lina." He started walking away, but then turned back. "I don't usually try to discourage my customers, but in your case, the grocery store in town has air conditioning."

Chapter 18

That evening, I scooted into a chair being held for me by Adam Cole, Pecan Bayou's newest district attorney. He brought me to Ben's Bayou, a restaurant built over the water of Pecan Bayou. It was the most expensive restaurant in town, although by big city standards, it probably wasn't all that unusual. In Pecan Bayou it was just nice to visit a restaurant that didn't feature a drive-through.

We sat at a table on the patio, right next to the water. I noticed a lack of mosquitoes and wondered if there was a stealth bug zapper working overtime somewhere.

"I was really surprised you decided to come to dinner with me tonight," he said.

He'd be surprised if he really knew why. "I figured you seemed like a nice guy, and well, I'm not getting any younger." That didn't come out right.

Adam Cole laughed and poured some white wine into my glass and then lifted his own for a toast. I quickly picked up my glass and clinked it to his.

"To new friends."

"To new friends," I repeated. I took a sip of my wine and looked out over the water. The sun would be setting in about an hour, and the heat was subsiding for the day. The cicadas chirped our dinner music along with the Willie Nelson ballad playing over the sound system.

"So how did you end up here in Pecan Bayou?" I asked.

"I don't know. Pecan Bayou is a small town, and it seemed like a nice place to settle down. I've always wanted to work in Texas, probably because I read too many Louis L'Amour novels. Anyway, when an opening came up here, I put in for it."

"I see. Well, we might be small, but we do have all kinds of crime."

"I've noticed that. I've only been here a week and we already have a murder and police harassment charge."

He brought it up. I didn't even have to reach for it.

"I heard about the murder, but what about police harassment?"

"Oh, some old cop was caught planting evidence at a crime scene. The local paper even had a picture of it. That one will be pretty open and shut."

I gulped my wine and then coughed.

"Are you all right?" he asked, getting up to pat me on the back.

"Yes," I gasped. "I'm fine." I pulled in a deep breath to continue the conversation. "You have a picture of the policeman actually holding evidence in his hand?"

"Well, no, you can't see evidence, but it's pretty clear what he's doing there."

This wasn't going well at all. He had already tried and convicted my dad.

"It seems to me you would need a lot more to go on that just some stupid picture."

Adam Cole leaned back in his chair and touched his fingertips together in front of him. "Betsy, you'll have to forgive me, but I really don't know all that much about you. What was it that you did for a living?"

"Uh, I'm a blogger."

"You make money at that? Blogging, I mean?"

"Enough. I just think that Lieutenant Kelsey needs a fair shake in all this, you know."

"I never said the officer's name," he said. "How would you know that? Is there something you haven't been telling me?"

Busted.

"I uh, read the papers like everyone else." I tried to make my light of my blunder.

"You said you hadn't heard about the harassment case."

"Excuse me?" A woman now stood next to our table holding on to a little girl who was wiggling to be free of her.

"Yes?" Adam turned.

"I couldn't help noticing you sitting here. You'll have to forgive me. My Daffodil here is going to be Miss Watermelon. Oops, that's not right." She placed her hand over her mouth and giggled, then began again. "Daffodil is going to be *in* the Miss Watermelon Pageant, and well, you are the judge ..."

Adam registered a blank look as he tried to comprehend what she just said. "You must have me mistaken for ..."

"Wait," I interrupted. "She's referring to me. I'm the judge."

Adam leaned in, "You're the judge?"

"Afraid so." I turned back to the woman, whose daughter was looking into the fish tank full of lobsters, tracing along the glass with her finger. She gently took her hand and led her over to the table. Daffodil curtsied.

"It is so nice to meet you," I said, "but I'm out to dinner right now with a friend. Could this wait for another time?"

The woman continued, "Oh, I can see you are out on a date, but we had heard that you had taken some time with some of the other contestants and thought this would only be fair."

"Oh. Well, actually I just ran into those girls, just like I seem to be running into you today. I'm sorry if you misunderstood. It's nice to meet you, Daffodil."

Daffodil looked up at me and smiled. "It is very nice to meet you." The lack of a contraction made me think it had been rehearsed.

"Well, thank you for your time," her mother said, starting to back away from the table.

The two walked away from the restaurant patio deck. With our view of the parking lot from the deck, I saw them climb in to a minivan. I wasn't sure if they had already had their meal or if they followed me here. How else would they know where to find me?

Adam smiled and picked up his wine, drinking it but never taking his eyes off of me. "So you're a beauty pageant judge. What do you blog about, fashion?"

"I write about helpful hints. You know, how to get out stains or keep refrigerator smelling fresh. That kind of stuff."

He snapped his fingers. "That's it! You're the Happy Hinter from the paper."

"You read my column?"

He shifted his weight to his other foot and smiled. "Well, okay. I've seen your column but have never actually read it. It's always on the page opposite the sports page."

"No wonder I have so many male readers."

"Hey, I'm sure there are women who read the sports page, too."

"Point taken."

The waiter approached us to take our orders and I was saved from further questions. I was turning out to be a lousy spy. I was supposed to be getting information out of him, but the more I talked the more I gave away.

"Hey, Miss Betsy." I looked up to see Keith Simmons, who used to be my paperboy. His grandfather was the owner of Simmons Hardware and had been the closest thing to a witness to Hunter Grayson's death. Keith had grown much taller than the twelve-year-old who would show up collecting his fee at my doorstep every month. His face was now suffering from the ravages of acne, and his body had turned into all arms and legs.

"Hi there, Keith. I didn't know you were working here," I said.

"Yes, ma'am. I've been here for a whole week now. Food service is my life now."

"That's great. Will you be working here during the school year?"

"I don't know, I sure would like to," he said. Keith took our order, writing each word down slowly and then repeating it back to us.

"Okay, so Betsy is having the gumbo," Keith said and then added with his best restaurant sales smile, "Good choice, Betsy ... and the gentleman you're with is having a steak, medium rare."

We both nodded, exhausted from his order-taking. After Keith left, I tried to redirect the conversation away from any connection Adam Cole might make from me to my father by bringing up the Fourth of July holiday.

"Will you be in town?"

"Yes, I guess so. It seems like too short of a holiday to really go anywhere. Do they have any fireworks here?"

"Oh, yes. Bubba McConnell lights them every year with the eight fingers he has left."

"Sounds like a night to remember – and now I can't wait to see the winner of the Miss Watermelon Pageant."

"There's a lot going on, that's for sure."

Keith came up to the table very slowly holding a giant round tray. He extended his serving stand and carefully set down our dinners. We became silent and put our napkins on our laps as he picked up my bowl of gumbo. It was filled to the very top with peppered broth, crawfish and okra. Right as Keith came closer with the teetering bowl a shot rang out, ricocheting on the metal frame of the patio. The bowl of gumbo came down on top of me and my dress as I heard Adam shout, "Get down!"

I hit the floor of the patio, trying to see where the shots were coming from. Okra flew everywhere. I saw a flash from trees and bushes situated next to the patio. The shooter was only twenty or so feet away, but as much as I tried to see I couldn't make out a person, only another flash of powder as the next shot rang out. I reached over to Keith, who was now lying on the ground next to me curled up in a ball.

Another shot hit a clay sun-shaped wall hanging that cracked and fell. The shards of clay shattered into pieces around us. Adam Cole was sprawled out on the other side of the table. There was blood dribbling over toward me. Adam had been hit. His face was turning a ghastly color of white. I reached over for my purse hanging from the chair and started dialing 911.

"Someone's been shot," I gasped.

I heard Keith moan beside me. I reached over and touched his arm. "Are you hurt too?"

"No," his adolescent voice squealed as it reached for its bass tone. "I'm beginning to think waiting tables isn't my calling, after all."

*****

The ambulance arrived about ten minutes after I called. When the shots had stopped, we slowly crawled back toward the inside of the restaurant. I followed the patch of blood on Adam and could see he had been hit in the arm. We pressed on the wound to stop the bleeding until help could arrive.

"New in town, and I'm already being shot at. Maybe that old cop has friends," Adam said. I felt guilt shoot through me. "He has more than that. You're out with his daughter."

"What?" he said, his voice still shaky.

"I'm Judd Kelsey's daughter."

A silence passed between us. "So you are here because of your father, not because you wanted to go out with me?"

I bit my lip. "I know, it's a bad thing to do, but I can tell you my father is an honest cop and he would never, ever plant evidence. You just have to believe me."

"And what were you prepared to do to make sure I did?"

I blushed. "Not what you're thinking."

If he wasn't sitting here bleeding all over me, I would have left him cold.

"Too bad," he said, using his good hand to straighten his shirt collar. "It's official. This is the worst date I have ever been on."

"It's on the top of my list, as well."

"So I just hope that wasn't your dad shooting at us."

"My dad's a better shot than that."

"Comforting."

"The shot was coming from over in the woods there," I said, motioning out the window.

"Did you see what the shooter looked like?" Adam was interrupted by the paramedics scrambling toward him. They started taking off his jacket and examining the gunshot wound.

"No, just the flash from the gun. There was lots of powder from it."

Keith, who had been clearing tables, stopped with a clatter. "My grandpa would say it's the ghost of Charlie Loper. That has to be it. Someone here must have hurt his daughter. He's a ghost out for revenge, you know."

"Who?" Adam asked.

"Oh," I sighed. "The shooting at the Loper mansion. His grandpa said he heard the gunshot and when he looked out the window he saw rhinestones flashing in the streetlight."

"I see," Adam said and then jumped as the paramedic started trying to get a look at his wound.

The paramedic stopped what he was doing and raised a finger. "It's a good thing you put pressure on the wound. You saved your friend from losing too much blood. If I could just get you to hold on to it for a minute more." He turned to pull something out of his medical kit and then turned back. As he was about to apply a bandage he stopped and looked into my face. "I know you. Orley's told me all about you. You're Betsy Livingston, the girl who has been at more of our stops than anyone in this town. Pleased to finally meet you," he said as he peeled up Adam's sleeve. He drew closer to the opening the bullet made. "I see an entrance and an exit on this. Looks like the bullet went right through you, sir. You were lucky." He whispered to him on the side, "Especially being out with this lady, if you know what I mean."

I pretended like I hadn't heard that part and focused on the bullet. Entering and exiting from his arm meant that it was probably still out on the patio somewhere.

"Betsy, we're going to transport your date to the hospital. Did you want to ride along?" the paramedic asked. "Oh, and you can let up with the pressure now."

I turned to answer his question when a flash lit in my eyes. It was Rocky with his camera.

"Smile, you're in the Gazette," he said. I always liked Rocky, but he was starting to get downright irritating.

"Rocky. I don't want to be in the Gazette."

"It's a major story, Betsy. Would you deny my readership? You know how low subscriptions are right now."

I turned back to Adam. "I know you're not too pleased with me right now, but I could drive your car to the hospital and park it in the parking lot."

He grimaced and reached for his keys in his front pocket. "That would be great." He handed them over. "I guess our date is over."

"Sure. I would say call me, but if the second date is anything like the first, it could be pretty frightening for both of us."

The paramedic loaded him onto the stretcher. Adam grasped onto the sides and said, "Besides, there is the little fact that you were pumping me for information on your father's case. I actually consider myself a fair judge of character, but I guess the apple doesn't fall far from the tree.

"Well, you can be pleased with yourself then, because you didn't reveal anything. No harm done," I said as I picked up my purse. The phone inside started ringing. The caller ID read "Dad."

Chapter 19

The next day, as he sat at my kitchen table ladling sauerkraut onto a hot dog, my father asked, "So did you see anything at all, Betsy?"

"I told you it was really difficult to see, but the shot was being fired from the brush near the bayou. There was a flash and some powder. Luckily, whoever it was wasn't a very good shot."

"We checked it out, and it's lookin' like they might have come from the antique Charlie Loper guns that were stolen from the museum."

"Okay, but after finding out that Hunter Grayson was funneling money off of Miss Loper, I can see a good reason for him to be killed. Shooting at me and Adam Cole is another matter." I said. "He's only been in town for a few weeks, so anybody wanting revenge for a case he tried seems a little soon. And me? Me? I'm the Happy Hinter. Who would want to take a shot at me for goodness' sake? What did I do, give some bad advice on ring around the collar?"

"Whatever you did, that gun was aimed right at you," my father answered.

"If I had to pick a suspect – and Dad, try not to take this personally – I think I would have to go with you. You have the biggest motive in town right now with Adam Cole investigating you."

"Which brings me to our next topic of conversation. What the hell were you doing out with him at Ben's Bayou?"

"Grandpa," Zach said. "You used a bad word. Mom said I can't say it, so why can you?"

"Listen to your mother, son," my dad said.

"Betsy, I need an answer to my question." His tone made me feel like I was sixteen sneaking into the house after curfew.

"Okay, okay. I know it probably wasn't a good idea, but I met him before I knew he was the new district attorney. He flirted with me a little and asked me out and I said no."

"Because she has a boyfriend," Zach said around a mouth full of sauerkraut.

"Right," I confirmed. "But then that thing came out about you in the paper, and they featured my picture of you. I just felt like I owed it to you. That's all."

Dad smiled and scooted closer. "Thank you for that," he paused, "but don't you ever do that again."

"Dad, it was no big deal. After we were shot at, I told him the truth. The worst that came out of it was that he disappointed I wasn't there for the right reason."

"Yeah, and he lives in this town now, and you don't want to go pissing off the district attorney."

"Grandpa!

"Sorry. So, in all of your spy work, did you find out anything?"

"No, he found out more about me than I did about his investigation," I admitted. "He described you as 'some old cop' who was caught planting evidence."

"Old? Now that hurts."

"That's what he said. I really wanted to get more out of him, but trying to question Mr. Cole was harder than I thought. Turns out I'm not as good at being sneaky as I thought."

Zach grinned while his cheeks bulged with hot dog.

"Who do you think would frame you like that, dad?" I said.

"You even have to ask? Clay Bonnet was yelling how I planted that pot even before I got out of the driveway with his son. It doesn't help that he's hired Irving Spalding to try his son's case. He'll get it thrown out of court before it ever comes to trial. It was just a stroke of good luck that Rocky heard about the charge and then looked through the pictures you brought in from the farm."

"Yeah, I used to think Rocky was on our side."

"He is, when it sells papers."

"But putting the picture in the paper without asking me or you and taking that picture at the restaurant?"

"It's his job, the same way you do yours and I do mine. He had a scoop."

My cell phone rang from behind me. My dad rose from the table and looked at the caller ID on the phone lying on the counter.

"It's Mr. Fitzpatrick, Betsy," he chuckled. "Wonder what he would think of your little dinner date?" He picked up his Stetson and headed for the door. "Have to run, darlin.'"

I answered the phone on the fourth ring.

"Betsy," Leo said, "are you all right?"

"Why wouldn't I be?"

"Well, maybe because you were just shot at."

"Oh, that."

"Yes that."

"How did you hear about that? It just happened."

"It's on the Internet," he said. "You made the statewide news."

"Oh," I said. "I'm okay. You don't need to worry. I wasn't even hit."

"It says someone else was. What were you doing there, anyway?"

Okay, here came the big confession. I would try to explain to him that I was really just on the date to get information on my dad's investigation. He would surely understand why I did what I did.

"Betsy?"

"Yes." I cleared my throat. "The man I was out with is the new district attorney in town. We met at the veterinarian's office. He has a dog named Sunshine."

"And you are...dating him?"

"No! Well, I was sort of ... but no, we won't be going out ever again."

"Being shot at kind of put him off, huh? No one ever said life with you would be easy." I could hear anger rising in Leo's voice.

"Let me explain."

"No need. You're a grown woman, and if you want to get picked up at the dog doctor, then have at it. I'll hand it to him – he does use his surroundings well. Who needs a bar when you can just take old Sunshine out for her shots?"

Now he was getting me angry. What did he think I was – available to anyone who asked? The idiot didn't even realize how I felt. I hadn't even defined it myself in my own head, but I sure wasn't shopping around for someone else to date.

"Leo..."

"Wow, look at the time. I'm just glad you're doing okay, Betsy."

The line went dead on the other end. He totally misunderstood what had happened and my reasons for being there. It surprised me that he reacted so quickly. Usually Leo was an excellent listener. It was one of the things I liked about him most. After my failed marriage, I felt like no one would ever pay any attention to me again. Leo didn't seem to be listening this time. If he had just stopped interrupting me, I could have gotten it out. I continued to worry about the situation as I did the lunch dishes and Zach ran out to play with Butch. I knew I had to do something, but I didn't think I could get Leo back on the phone. I walked over to the computer and started writing an email to "weatherguy." My weatherguy.

"I'm so sorry about this misunderstanding. I am not sending love letters to Adam Cole, the new district attorney. It was all a big mix-up. As if I would send anything nice to the guy who is framing my father..."

I noticed that when I pulled up my email, there had been a message from Dr. Springer. It started to gnaw at me that possibly something had come back from the blood test she took after Butch's week in "captivity."

Putting off writing to Leo, I clicked back to my inbox and opened the email from Dr. Springer.

Dear Clients of Springer Veterinary Clinic,

To celebrate the Fourth of July this year, we are having our first pet parade before the beauty pageant. Dress your dog or cat in their finest patriotic outfit and join the parade at the Pecan Bayou Public Park! Hope to see you there!

I looked back at the list of recipients of the email and noticed Adam Cole's name near the beginning. Would he be there with Sunshine? He left the restaurant pretty angry with me. I was hoping that he would understand a daughter helping out her father, but instead I probably once again made matters worse for my dad. Maybe I would go down to his office to try to smooth things out. Then again, maybe I should just let it go.

It probably wouldn't hurt to write him a little email and apologize for making a fake date with the man. I started a new email to Adam, leaving the email to Leo unsent. I was feeling scatterbrained about the whole thing and just had the overwhelming impulse to fix it all, right now. I would write him a note first and then transfer his email address from Dr. Springer's list to this new email.

Hey, sorry about our date, and not just the shooting. I think you're a really great guy...

Zach burst through the back door with Butch. His face was the color of ripe watermelon.

"Man, it's hot out there. Can I have a soda?" He looked like the poster boy for sunstroke, so I jumped up and poured him some water with ice in it. I wet a kitchen towel and put it on the back of his neck.

"What about Butch?" he asked. Bossy for a kid. I put some fresh water in Butch's bowl, which he lapped up until it was gone.

"You should have come in sooner, Zach. This heat can be dangerous."

"Sorry, Mom, but we were exploring,'" Zach said after gulping down another mouthful of water. Zach tried to put the wet cloth on the back of Butch's neck, but the dog pulled away from him and went over to the braided rug in the den and collapsed, panting.

"Poor boy, he's all worn out."

The gray puppy looked tired, but at the same time in a state of euphoria only achieved from playing with a little boy on a hot summer day.

The back door swung open again, and Danny came clomping into the room.

"Betsy! We're going to have a parade! We're going to have a parade!"

"Yes, I know, Danny. I was just reading about it in an email the doctor sent."

"We're going to have a parade with dogs! Dr. Springer says we can bring Butch and have him in the parade." Aunt Maggie had followed her son in quietly and was now pulling a water bottle out of my refrigerator. After she unscrewed the cap and took a swig, she sighed.

"They've decided to have a dog parade to celebrate the Fourth. They're going to put them in the front of the regular parade so as not to spook the dogs. Dr. Springer's telling all her clients to dress up their pets."

"Not the cat people. They're not invited. Cats don't parade good, you know," Danny added.

"Cool!" Zach said. "Can you make Butch a little flag costume?"

"I don't know about that, but we can do something."

"We could attach sparklers to his collar."

"I know, I can make Butch a red, white and blue yo-yo outfit," said Aunt Maggie. My aunt was famous for her yo-yo bedspreads, and we each had one. She loved to take little scraps and turn them into puffy circles that she would then sew onto a bedspread. It was only fitting that Butch should have his own.

"I'm going to meet my girlfriend there," Danny said. I shot Aunt Maggie a look. I guessed Allison would be there, but how comfortable would she feel with Danny professing his love to her in front of the crowd.

Maggie raised her eyebrows and shook her head. She knew a heartbreak was coming for her son. She attempted to change the subject.

"I'm sure Adam Cole will be there with that dog of his. What's his name? Aquarius?"

"Sunshine," I said. "If he is there, he probably doesn't want to talk to me. He wasn't too happy when he found out I was Judd Kelsey's daughter."

"I suppose not. That's alright, you tried."

"Unfortunately, Leo heard about it and wasn't too happy on the phone."

I had never seen Leo angry. More than angry, he had seemed hurt. It had been such a simple idea to go and get some answers out of the man who was investigating my father on a false charge. Now the simple idea had turned into a bad situation with a man that I was pretty sure I had some strong feelings for. I didn't know if I was ready to head for the love thing, but being with Leo was just easy and felt right. My time with Leo was not something I wanted to lose in my life because of one dinner date.

"You had better call him and make it right, Betsy. Fellas like that don't mosey into your life every day," said Maggie.

I knew she was right and just had to hope he would read my email. I returned to my computer to go back to the email I had started.

"Mom!" I heard from the next room. "Do we have any more hot dogs?"

When I became a parent, I never knew my life would turn into the job of a 24-hour waitress who never earned a single tip. I quickly filled in both the men's emails and sent them off.

That night as I worked on my next column on fireworks anxiety and dogs, I checked my inbox to see if there was an email from Leo. If there was just a way I could get him to listen to me, then I could explain everything.

My phone rang. This had to be Leo and my chance to set things straight. I grabbed for it.

A male voice on the other end started the conversation before I could say hello. "Uh, Betsy. This is the guy who is trying to frame your father."

I recognized a voice that was now becoming familiar on the other side of the line. Would this ever end? How many times could I insult this man and get away with it?

"Adam?" I know I had said it, but never to his face.

"That's me. I just received your email." His tone was curt and to the point. "Look, although I'm not from around these here parts, I will treat your father's case with fairness. Just because somebody makes a claim, it doesn't necessarily mean it's the truth. You should realize I've been around long enough to know that."

I slowly came to the realization that he was reacting to the email I sent Leo. Had I accidentally switched the email addresses of Adam and Leo? That would mean ... I ran to my computer, phone in hand, and checked my "sent" mail. Sure enough, I had done the unthinkable.

Adam sounded like a pretty nice guy even if he was a major force of stress in my family's life. He also seemed like the kind of guy I really would have dated if I hadn't already met Leo. He was the kind of guy my dad would like. Somehow I had injured him further, and I knew I had to make it right.

"I'm so glad you said that," I replied. "That's all I ask is that you examine both sides of the complaint. You have to admit, just because he's leaning over in that picture it doesn't mean he's planting evidence."

"Point taken."

"Thank you, and – well, I'm sorry for trying to trick you, and you should know that email was meant for someone else."

"You mean the boyfriend your son keeps bringing up?"

"Oh, you know about that, huh?"

"Small-town news travels fast."

"Well, I'm sorry I went about it all the way I did, but you just have to understand this is my dad we're talking about."

"And if you had mentioned that from the beginning, we would have had this very conversation a whole lot sooner."

"Just probably not on a date."

"Where someone might be shooting at us."

Relief flooded through me as he continued, "Do you have any idea who our gunman might be?"

"No, but..." I hesitated to add this next part. "I know you were bleeding and all, but did you hear our waiter telling me he thought it was the ghost of Charlie Loper? The whole town thinks Charlie is out shooting anyone who has anything to do with his daughter."

"So who was he shooting at? You or me?"

"Who knows, but there are witnesses now who say they actually saw him out there on the bank with his golden Colts."

"Do you know the names of these people?" he asked.

"Not directly," I said. "It's just on the town gossip hotline."

"How do I get that number?"

"Go get your hair done down at Ruby Green's Best Little Hair House in Texas," I told him.

"Sorry, I like my present style. You didn't see any old cowboys in the woods, did you?"

"No, I saw smoke, and the light caught on something out there. The police checked the area where they think the shooter was standing and didn't find anything much."

"Of course not, don't they know apparitions don't leave footprints?"

"My dad did tell me that they had our new crime scene photographer go out and take pictures of the shooting location."

"I'll check with the police department and see if I can look at the photos. What's the name of this guy?"

"Elena Morris."

"Oops, how sexist of me," he said. "My mother would have a fit if she heard that."

"So, are we all right, even with my many blunders?" I asked.

"I'm not sure at this point," he said. "Just don't give up your writing job. You make a sorry undercover cop."

Chapter 20

"Okay, so Betsy, you got all this straight, right?" asked Rocky as we walked around the Pecan Bayou park that had been transformed into a watermelon festival carnival with a beauty pageant platform. The gazebo side of the park had been decorated with red and blue bunting hung from every corner, and a portable stage had been set up on one side as a runway. I was joined by Stan, the manager from NUTV, Rocky from the paper and Tory Parker, a local dance teacher. Tory would be the other judge – someone who was much more qualified than I was in deciding the fate of all these little girls and their parents. Stan planned to have his crew out filming the entire pageant. He was also the unofficial producer/stage manager.

"Uh, basically the little girls walk down the runway, and I judge them for poise and style." I said, imagining the contestants on the assembled stage.

"And confidence," Stan added, straightening the hem of his Geoffrey Beene summer plaid shirt. His watch was circled by tiny diamonds that shone against the pristine black of the dial. He had started using mousse in his hair, which now stood up in small spikes at the front.

"Right, confidence. Gotcha."

"We are looking for the complete package. A girl with style, poise and that special something," Tory added.

"We really appreciate you helping us with the judging duties for this," Rocky said. He should be grateful, seeing as he had personally pushed my dad toward an unfair investigation. He knew our friendship was greatly strained and was being overly solicitous to me to make up for it.

Rocky grinned and continued. "And don't forget to pick a cute one. That'll photograph well in the Gazette."

Tory Parker's carefully lined eyes started to cross. To her a beauty pageant was an invitation to style, not a front-page "aww, gee" moment.

"What if they're all cute? All of the little girls I've seen so far were cute," I said.

"Then you need another criterion for judging. Something that you are looking for in a contestant," Stan said.

"And what would that be?" I asked.

"I don't know, Betsy. It's up to you on that one. Use your judgment."

He really thought I knew what I was doing. He had always overestimated my abilities, dating back to the time he asked me to do a fifteen-minute weekly segment on helpful hints a couple of years ago. Even though now I appeared on "Betsy's Helpful Hints" every week and had a following of sorts, it took me a few times to get it right. I just wasn't all that comfortable being in front of a camera, until Leo gave me some pointers. I talked about cleaning tips, organization and recipes, and Stan received an occasional letter or email from viewers with questions. It didn't hurt that I had my giant database of household hints and tips that I had collected over the years.

"And you are going to do all the master of ceremony stuff, right Stan?" I asked.

"Oh yes, I have my tuxedo out of mothballs, and I'm ready to officiate."

"Just promise me you're not going to sing," Rocky said flatly.

Tory Parker straightened the fold on her red slacks, and the diamond ring given to her by her husband, a much older man, glimmered in the light. She laid her lacquered red fingernails on Rocky's arm. "Honestly, Mr. Whitson, do we want the Little Miss Watermelon going down the runway with no music behind her? It would be ghastly."

"Just what is the official watermelon song, anyway?" I asked.

Stan tapped his chin. "There isn't one yet. Seeing as this is our first pageant, we'll have to think of one or maybe even have Waylon write one for us." Waylon Rodriguez was our local country music talent. He played out at Tipsy's every Friday night. I couldn't wait to hear what that song would sound like.

"You do know I've been confronted by most of the contestants and their mothers, don't you?"

"More than what I saw at the Gazette? I certainly hope you haven't made any promises," said Rocky.

"I'm trying, but they don't make it easy."

Tory laughed. "Ah yes, the perils of the job. When I was running for Miss Hill Country in 1995, my mother parked outside one of the judges' houses for two days just so she could be on the same jogging path."

Stan laughed. "Now that's dedication."

I heard a rustle behind us. After all this time, I was beginning to be able to identify the enemy just by sound. I took a look behind me for anyone dragging along a little girl in taffeta.

A woman and her daughter smiled and waved, and then she lifted the little girl up onto the runway and started coaching her on walking techniques. The little girl, even though she seemed to be listening to her mother never once took her eyes off of our little group. It was more than a little creepy. She grinned as if she had been born with that facial expression and then took a special sashay in our direction. Her mother's praise traveled across the field to us.

"Deciding is going to be tough," Tory said.

Stan glanced at his watch, that black dial encircled by diamonds. It was a little flashier than most of his wardrobe, and it looked expensive. "You just choose who you think is right. I've got to run."

"I, too, must leave," Tory said, grabbing her bag. "I have a tap class in less than an hour. See you on Saturday, Betsy. Oh, and be sure to dress up a little. It makes it more special for the girls." What, my jean shorts and tank top wouldn't work?

Stan and Tory's exit left Rocky and me alone together for the first time since he put my father's picture in the paper.

"Uh, listen Betsy," Rocky started. Here it came, his apology and a promise of a retraction on the accusations made against my father. He stumbled a bit over his words, a surprising thing from someone who used vocabulary so well. "I just want you to know that even though I put that picture in the paper, I don't have anything against your dad. If I had to call this one, he's probably innocent."

"Probably?"

"Sure. I've known your dad for years, and he's never done anything like planting evidence."

"Then why did you say he did?"

"They say a picture is worth a thousand words, and well, I had the picture, thanks to you."

"Did it matter to you that you might get my father fired?"

"Of course it did, but you just have to understand that when it comes to news I have to follow my gut."

"Well your gut," I said, picking up my purse and slinging it over my shoulder, "sucks."

"Before you question my motives, darlin', I suggest you look at your own. I would like to ask just what you were doing out for a cozy little dinner with the district attorney handling your father's investigation?"

"Is this on the record or off the record?" I said. Before Rocky could reply, I stopped him. "Oh yes, I forgot, it's all up to your gut. Well, for your information, Adam Cole had no idea I was Judd Kelsey's daughter."

Rocky's eyebrows raised. "Why Betsy, you surprise me. You were trying to pull one off on Adam Cole."

"Don't be too surprised. He didn't know until the guy started shooting."

"And I know I asked you this, but did you see the guy?"

"Nope, just some smoke, and ... something sparkled."

"Sparkled?"

"That's what I said. We have a notorious, sparkly killer, right here in Pecan Bayou."

Chapter 21

"Come on boy," Zach said as he pulled Butch down the street. Even though Butch seemed happy at home with us, when freedom beckoned, he was willing to listen. He started wriggling out of the red white and blue yo-yo-laden collar Aunt Maggie had made him. To compliment the collar, he wore a dog-sized sailor hat with blue stars on the brim. No matter what, it seemed to stay on, and I just had to hope Zach and Danny hadn't super-glued it to Butch's head.

"Zach, hold on to him." Children and adults surrounded us, each holding their patriotically decorated pooches. Dr. Springer and Allison were trying to put the dogs and their owners into a line. This effort worked pretty well until a fight occurred between a Lady Liberty dachshund and an Uncle Sam shih tzu. I never did imagine that those two characters would actually like each other.

"Mom, Butch is too strong. I can't hold him." Butch pulled on his new blue nylon leash, twisting it as he wrapped himself around Zach. I grabbed the leash from Zach's small hands and unwound the dog from my son.

"Betsy," said Dr. Springer. "If I could get you and Butch over here?" Betsy and Zach followed the doctor's orders.

"And Mr. Cole, why don't you and Sunshine walk behind them?" Dr. Springer seemed pretty pleased with herself for putting the two of us next to each other. She had only seen the picture in the paper and couldn't have known we weren't actually dating. Adam Cole smiled stiffly and stood behind us.

"Dr. Springer!" A woman came running up behind us with a little girl. The dog, a white poodle, was reluctant to enter the parade line, and the woman had to drag him over. "We would like to stand next to Mrs. Livingston and her dog. He's just a puppy, and our Noodles does well around puppies. Noodles can be a bit obstinate." She turned toward me and extended a hand. "How do you do? I'm Mellie Nicholson, and this

110

here is my granddaughter, Nora. She's here visiting us for the Fourth, and when we saw the pageant in the paper, I just had to put her in it." After finishing this sentence, Mellie Nicholson's face froze in a smile as she gestured toward her granddaughter. The way she flourished her hands over the child, I felt like I was looking at a brand-new car on The Price is Right.

Nora looked up at me, her expression a contrast to her grandmother's. She flatly announced, "This is Noodles," and pointed to the dog she was holding.

Noodles was a white poodle with red striped ribbons on his ears. Noodles didn't seem to be the least bit interested in whatever dog he was put next to, but his owner sure wanted to be next to me.

"That's okay, Dr. Springer. Why don't Sunshine and I go to the back of the line?" said Cole. "We don't mind bringing up the rear." Following a bunch of dogs who thought they were going for a walk, I thought Adam Cole a brave man. He guided Sunshine to the back of the line, which was now stretching around the corner.

"Betsy!" Danny came running over to us. He almost ran into Allison, who had walked over to pet Noodles. Danny shuffled his feet and blushed.

He took in a big breath and came out with, "Hi, Allison."

"Hi, Danny," Allison returned, smiling sweetly. No wonder he thought he was in love with her. It was like she didn't see his disability at all.

"This is Betsy's dog, Butch," he informed her.

"I know. I remember Butch. He's the only dog we've had that was kidnapped this year."

"Right," said Danny. Allison patted Danny on the back and then walked over to a barking schnauzer to settle him down.

"She's pretty," said Zach, now folding his arms and watching Allison walk away. My son looked like a barfly checking out the night's catch.

"Zach," I said, "maybe she's smart, too."

"She's real smart," said Danny, a quiver in his voice. Would she break his heart when he found out she didn't feel about him the way he felt about her? I knew I needed to apply the redirect strategy.

"Do you like Butch's costume?" I asked him.

Mellie Nicholson cut in. "I think it's lovely and full of imagination."

"Thank you," said Zach. "My aunt helped make it, but I dressed him myself." He beamed.

Nora Nicholson pushed up her glasses. Her skinny legs poked out of a white sundress with a blue stripe on the bottom and red bows on the straps. "It looks like it came from the drugstore to me," she said, bluntly popping my son's balloon of pride.

Zach, not one to back down in a fight, responded, "What would you know about it? Your dog's name is Noodles. Who names their dog after spaghetti?"

The little girl took off her glasses and calmly placed them in her pocket. I couldn't be sure, but I think she was about to punch my son in the nose. She was a year or two younger than Zach and also a prospective Little Miss Watermelon, so I stepped between them.

"Noodles is a fine name." I stared down at Zach. "Right?"

Zach's gaze wavered from the girl to me to the girl. "Sure," he muttered. Butch started to pull on the leash again.

"Is that my Scout?" Libby Loper came up to us through the crowd of trained dogs and untrained people. She bent down to Butch's level and whistled. Butch ran to her pulling Zach behind him. The puppy licked her face as she laughed. Today she had on a white straw Stetson and blue leather vest with red trimming on it. She had regained the pride of the little girl on the white horse.

"His name is Butch," Zach insisted.

"I know, dear, I know," she said gently. "Your Butch here was the first friend I made after a long time of feeling alone. I hope you don't mind an old lady being a little grateful."

"Well, if you put it that way. You can call him Scout if you want to. I don't mind."

Libby put her arm around Zach's shoulder and squeezed. "Thank you, dear, and I hope I have made another friend," she said. She released Zach and scratched behind the puppy's ear, bracelets clinking. I looked up at the front of the line and saw Clay and Lina Bonnet with their giant Rottweiler, Outlaw. I know that if I asked, Dr. Springer would tell me that not all Rottweilers are vicious dogs, but the Bonnets' dog just looked mean. People would walk by him and he would snarl his lip up on one side and begin to growl.

Pastor Green, Ruby's brother from the Pecan Bayou Community Church, smiled and attempted to approach the Bonnets. Their dog growled, and the pastor dropped his hand and hurried away. Just like the Bonnets, this dog was nothing to be trifled with. The more I watched them, the more I was sure they had lied about my dad. Clay Bonnet jerked the dog back into line while Lina fanned herself with a paper fan.

"Checking out your plaintiffs?" I was not aware that Adam Cole was once again standing right behind me. The scent of aftershave drifted my way as he spoke over my shoulder.

"Huh? No – well, maybe. I was just noticing how mean their dog was."

"Not all dogs reflect their owners, you know."

"That's good, because I would never nickname you Sunshine."

Elena Morris came running up, leading a brown and white border collie on a leash. "Am I late?" she asked. Elena looked different out of uniform with jean shorts and a red halter top on. She actually looked like a normal person, not the pushy photographer I had met last week.

"Not yet," I answered.

"Nice to meet you," Adam Cole extended his hand. "I'm Adam."

"Elena."

"Adam, this is the crime scene photographer and the newest member of the Pecan Bayou police force."

"Oh, then we have some things to talk about. I'm the district attorney and one of the people who was shot." He reached up and touched his arm. I could see the edge of a bandage sticking out from the sleeve of his shirt.

"You can get in line behind me and Sunshine," he told her. Watching them walk to the back of the line, I felt a little less guilty about tricking him into dinner.

An eardrum-piercing squeal came from the flag-strewn platform.

"Ladies and gentlemen ... and dogs." The mayor of Pecan Bayou stood up front, the mic towering over him. Our mayor was a giant of a man, figuratively speaking. Elmer Obermeyer fancied himself a baseball superfan, and many of his campaign speeches were riddled with baseball metaphors. "Let's hit it out of the park! Vote for me, and it's a home run!" Elmer went to high school with Nolan Ryan years back and made sure everyone knew they still stayed in touch.

"We're about to start our parade down Main Street. Now, Benny's Barbecue has agreed to close their doors for the duration of the parade so we don't get any stragglers. Is everybody ready to parade?"

The crowd murmured in agreement. "Then let's play ball!" he shouted. He pushed a button on a CD player that was hooked up to the speakers in the park, and we started walking to "Stars and Stripes Forever," heading to a crowd of people now standing on the street or relaxing in lawn chairs. The Bonnets led the way with Clay holding on to Outlaw and Lina holding a sign that said "Bonnet Farms." I had never thought of this as a way to advertise.

I could see my dad and George Beckman standing near the end of the parade route, ready to direct us around the corner. Even though my dad was on "limited duty" as the paper put it, over the tourist-packed holiday, there seemed to be no such thing. As we entered the official parade route, I noticed that all of the old downtown buildings were open for business. Maybe they hoped for a freak "middle of the summer even though it's hot as heck" sale. Aunt Maggie sat in her white folding lawn chair in front of Earl's. When she saw us in the parade she waved and cheered us on.

The heat bore down on us, and the sun was almost blinding our view. The dogs panted in unison, leaving trails of drool on the ground. Some of the old buildings had large upstairs windows and balconies to let in fresh air, a feature left over from the pre-air conditioning days. I couldn't imagine living in Texas before the advent of air conditioning and didn't know how people survived. It would have meant night after night of no sleep, tossing and turning in the muggy heat. No wonder they kept shouting "Remember the Alamo!" The people back then were so exhausted they had to remind each other.

Noodles and family who were now in front of us started moving. I nudged Butch, Zach and Danny to start moving. Zach and Danny had been practicing their princess waves just for the parade. They were politely holding up two fingers and waving them in the air to their adoring subjects. The music on the CD switched to the 1812 Overture, complete with cannon fire. The heat of the sun was relentless, and I was beginning to visualize a really nice tall glass of iced tea. A sparkle caught my eye as I squinted into the sun, and then I saw a cowboy standing up on the balcony above Simmons Hardware Store. He raised his gun, and I knew immediately that this was a repeat of my dinner date.

"Look, Mom, there's a cowboy up there," Zach said. Many of the other paraders looked up and pointed.

"Free ice cream at Earl's Java!" I yelled, and the paraders and crowd all rose and crowded into sleepy Earl's establishment. Children and dogs headed for the door with the coffee bean nested in a big E. I heard a shot and then a dog yelp but continued to push the boys out of the street.

The figure on the balcony was gone and then instantly reappeared across the street in another window. I waited for him to shoot, but he didn't raise his hands from his sides. The cowboy just stood there looking out at us.

"Betsy, can we get ice cream?" Danny asked. I looked up into the window again, but now there was nobody there.

Out in the street I could see Noodles lying on the pavement, blood running from him. George Beckman walked into the street, speaking into his shoulder walkie, "Poodle down, please advise."

Then I heard my dad crackling through the static on the other end, "Dammit George, forget the dog and try to find the shooter."

Chapter 22

"I'm tryin' to tell you folks, I don't serve ice cream here. This is a coffee shop," Earl said, wiping his hands on his apron.

"But they said free ice cream."

"Who said it?"

I pulled the boys back toward the doorway.

"Where's Mama?" Danny asked.

"I don't know."

"I have to find Mama," Danny said.

"No, we need to stay here until Uncle Judd tells us it's safe."

"Is he with Mama?"

"Probably." I had no idea where my father was or if Maggie was with him. Having Danny walking around out there was not an option. He outweighed me by about 60 pounds, and stopping him would have been difficult. After losing his father, Danny's greatest fear was losing his mom.

"Oh! My Noodles!" Mellie Nicholson cried from behind me. "Why did he have to go and shoot Noodles?" Much to Earl's relief, the assembled crowd turned their attention to her and her granddaughter. They were still unaware of anything other than free ice cream. Had the shooter wanted to kill the dog? I was beginning to become leery of duded-up cowboys. I wondered if I hadn't been the object of the shooter, who just happened to be a lousy shot.

"It was the ghost of Charlie Loper," one old man said in the crowd. "I recognized his six gun. He's back to right the wrong perpetrated against his daughter by this town."

People all around him whispered in agreement. "He'll not rest until he searches out the wrongdoers."

"Wait a minute," I said, raising my hand before the man procured a posse and a hanging rope. "If he is after the wrongdoers, wouldn't that have been Hunter Grayson, the butler who was stealing from her? Why would he randomly target a poodle in the parade?"

"Don't know, but he was shooting at Ben's Bayou Restaurant just a few days ago."

"Betsy was there, she knows about that," Danny volunteered. The crowd's eyes now turned toward me.

The old man's bony finger extended across the room to me. "It's you! You're the one the ghost wants. What have you done to his daughter? Were you in cahoots with the butler?"

I could feel the crowd moving in on me even though no one had taken a step. My grasp on Zach tightened.

"First of all, there's no such thing as a ghost who shoots live bullets. Second, I didn't even know that woman lived in that house until our dog crawled under her gate."

"That's it. Charlie Loper thinks you stole her dog."

Zach squared off with his hands on his hips. "We never stole that dog. She stole him from us."

"Yeah," Danny said, duplicating Zach's pose.

"How could you?" Mellie Nicholson said. "How could you endanger all of us with your petty squabble with a ... ghost?"

"We need to get away from this woman. She's raised the ire of the ghost," the old man said, pointing that bony finger my way. In silent agreement, the people rose from the floor and started leaving the store, glancing back at us.

"I don't think it's safe to leave yet," I said.

"It's a hell of a lot safer than being around you," said the old man. He picked up his dachshund, decorated like a hot dog, and hugged it to his chest.

As the people started toward the doorway, it became filled with my father and George, standing there blocking their way.

"Sorry, folks. I'm going to have to ask you to stay for just a few more minutes," my father said.

"It's not safe here. That woman is going to get us all killed!" one woman shrieked. "We have to get the children out."

"What woman?" my father asked. They all turned and pointed to me. My father smiled and nodded.

"I think you're safe, but why would being around her make you targets?"

"Because," Nora Nicholson said, "obviously if you had been paying attention, Officer, you would have put together the clues that this lady is the person the cowboy was trying to hit. He tried to kill her at the restaurant and now in the parade. It's her fault that the cowboy ghost shot my grandma's dog."

"Ya know, you got a point there," Judd drawled. "Still, I need to ask you-all some questions." With that the crowd collectively groaned, and I started to feel a little less like I was about to be lynched.

"I saw the ghost of Charlie Loper up on the balcony over at Simmons Hardware," a man in the crowd said.

"No," said another woman, "he was in the window over the locksmith shop. It was clear as day."

"No, no, he's right," said Nora. "I saw him too, and it was over Simmons Hardware where Santa Claus stands every year at Christmas."

"Dad," I said, "not to complicate things any more than I have already, but I saw him in both places – first over the hardware store and then over the locksmith shop."

"How long in between those two sightings?"

"That's the weird part. I saw him over the hardware store. Then, only seconds later, he was over the locksmith store."

"Did he have a gun?"

"I saw one when he was over the hardware store," I said. "When he was in the upper window of the locksmith shop, he just stood there with his arms to his side, and the next time I looked he was gone."

"Ghosts can't hold their earthly orbs for too long, you know," my Aunt Maggie said, pushing her way through the door.

"Mama!" shouted Danny, who jumped up and hugged her small form.

"You knew I'd find you bubby," she said. "Besides, I knew you were safe and sound with Betsy and Zach."

"And Butch. Don't forget Butch," Danny said, smiling.

Maggie turned to face the crowd. "I am a member of the Pecan Bayou Paranormal Society, and I can tell you that Charlie Loper probably expended all of his energy just shootin' at that poor unfortunate dog."

The crowd nodded, respecting the expert in the room. Too bad I didn't quite agree with her theory. Where does a ghost get a gun? The haunted pawn shop?

"Maggie," my father said. "Did you see this cowboy?"

"Yes, I did. He appeared to me as a full apparition over Simmons Hardware."

"Did you see him on the other side?"

"No, sorry to say, that was all I experienced."

"What about Noodles?" Mellie Nicholson said.

George cut in. "Don't worry, ma'am. We're finding Dr. Springer to see to your dog. Someone said she ran back to the clinic to get something right before the parade."

I hadn't seen Dr. Springer since the beginning of the parade when she was lining us up. I would have thought she would have stayed to see the parade she worked so hard to organize. Hopefully she would get to Noodles soon, but from the looks of the dog, the bullet had ended its life. A few inches more and it might have been me laying out that street. I shivered at the thought of it. Had the shooter been trying to get me? And if so, what for? I had never done anything but discover Hunter Grayson. Maybe it was really the ghost of Hunter Grayson back to get me for climbing his stupid fence.

Now that the crowd had settled down and begun to disperse, I gathered Zach and Butch to leave. Maggie and Danny followed behind us. How could the shooter be on both sides of the street at the same time? Was there really a pistol-packing ghost out there? It almost made me want to believe it. That was the easiest theory.

As we entered Main Street I saw several others straggling out of the stores and folding up chairs. Mayor Obermeyer was straightening his toupee as Rocky Whitson was attempting to get a "man on the street" interview from him for the paper. Benny's Barbecue had reopened its doors, no longer worrying about dogs straying in. Several people were now rocking in the rocking chairs usually filled by tourists, drinking sweet tea and fanning themselves in the heat.

Noodles was still in a sad heap in the street. From behind me, Mellie Nicholson and her granddaughter ran out to their dog. A mournful wail came from Mellie as she approached the dog.

"Betsy. Will the white dog be all right?" Danny asked.

"I don't think so, Danny."

"What's wrong with him?"

"Don't worry about him," Aunt Maggie said. "Dr. Springer will do all she can for the dog, but sometimes..."

I looked up to the balcony where the cowboy shooter had stood. It couldn't have really been the ghost of Charlie Loper. Whoever it was had to have entered through Simmons Hardware and then taken the stairs in the back behind the windshield wiper display.

"We were lucky," Zach said. "It could have been Butch. Just what did Charlie Loper have against dogs anyway?"

I didn't stop to correct him and to acknowledge what was going on in my head. Charlie Loper – or whoever it was – hadn't been aiming for the dog. He had been aiming for me.

"Are you okay?" Adam Cole came from around the corner holding the leashes of both Sunshine and Elena Morris's border collie.

"Yes, we're fine," I said, "but the dog in front of us was shot. Where is Elena? Is she all right?" Adam glanced out into the street where Noodles was awaiting veterinary assistance.

"Elena is fine. She had to work the scene, so she handed me her dog. You know, Betsy, nothing personal, but I'm really glad I got bumped in line. Being next to you seems to be a dangerous thing."

"Yes, I need to put that on my dating profile – 'draws sniper fire.'"

"Well, look, the two of you are together again and there's a shooting!" Rocky snapped a picture, leaving a flash trailing across my eyeballs.

"Rocky, I hate to disappoint you, but Adam and I were not standing together this time."

"That's okay," he said. "The town will want to know what local celebrities were victims to the specter of Charlie Loper."

"Really? That's the headline you're going with, Rocky?"

"Ghosts sell papers, sweetheart."

"Ghosts don't shoot guns," I said.

"Nope, but that's not my problem." Rocky started walking away with his camera.

I shouted after him. "Rocky, I don't give you my permission to use that picture! The last one got me in trouble with..." I stopped cold. Did I really want to announce my relationship status across Main Street?

"With whom?" Adam asked.

"With ... oh ... It's none of your business."

I turned and discovered that Maggie had taken Danny, Zach and the puppy into the ice cream parlor, which was now having the biggest rush in its history of doing business. I knew Maggie was probably trying to get her son and nephew away from the now-dead corpse of Noodles. I turned back to Adam.

"I need to go," I said and started walking across the street to Simmons Hardware.

"You know, Betsy, now that I've been here a while, I've started hearing stories about you," he said.

"Not all bad, I hope."

"No, but you do seem to run across an inordinate amount of crime scenes. I don't know whether to arrest you or put you on the payroll."

"Money's always nice," I said and ducked into Simmons. I made my way to the back of the store and tried the door to the stairs. I had never really been up the stairs before, although I had seen the door open from time to time. I shot up the stairs and found a storeroom with boxes stacked high containing various auto repair manuals. I squirmed through them and found Pecan Bayou crime scene tape stretched across the doors that led to the balcony. Here we were in small-town Texas with our very own book depository crime scene. I didn't need to see so much where the shooter stood but needed to know how he could have gotten from one side of the street to the other so quickly. I glanced at the second hand on my watch and started down the stairs and took the back alley behind the store. From there I ran around the other store. The only way I could get across the street in a hurry would be to actually cross the street. The ghost of Charlie Loper would have stuck out in full cowboy garb. There was no way a shooter could get from one side to the other in that amount of time.

"Betsy." I recognized my father's voice from behind me. "What are you doing?"

"Trying to figure out how whoever shot at us ended up in two places at once."

My father sighed. "Yeah, well, just don't get in the way." He paused and then admitted, "Actually, I've been doing the same thing."

"I just tried timing it, and it would have taken at least two minutes to cross the street and go up the stairs on the other side."

"There's no explaining it," my father said.

"Unless it was truly the ghost of Charlie Loper." Aunt Maggie stood behind us with a fresh cone of rocky road ice cream.

Chapter 23

The next morning I woke up with a slight headache, which became less slight when I saw the special Saturday edition of the Pecan Bayou Gazette.

"Town Victims of Crazed Ghost!" screamed the headline. Rocky had filled the front page with eyewitness interviews, pictures of people in the parade, pictures of dogs in the parade, and of course his celebrity corner with me, Adam and the mayor. Today's paper would have made The Enquirer envious. Too bad we didn't have Elvis's alien baby in the parade. That would have sold a few copies.

The town of Pecan Bayou was hoping for a big turnout for the Watermelon Festival. With a front page like this, we might have to rent more port-a-potties. Leo had talked about coming down for the festival, but after our last conversation I wasn't counting on it. He'd seemed pretty mad, and then my switching the emails between him and Adam probably finished off my last chance at having a fulfilling relationship in my life. Maybe if I tried to call him, I could sort some things out.

I started to reach for my cell phone but then heard the squeak of my back door opening. Could this be him now, ready to forgive and forget? So what if he had pictorial proof of my dating another man behind his back. So what if he had an email proof of my pursuit of another guy. Anyone could get past that, right?

"Betsy?"

"In here, Dad," I said.

"Is Zach up yet?"

"No, I was letting him sleep. After all the excitement yesterday, he had a hard time settling down last night."

"Two scoops of bubble gum ice cream probably didn't hurt too much, either."

"Did you see the paper? Rocky has gone tabloid on us."

"Yes, I did. We called over some relief help from Andersonville for today. We just don't know what to expect."

"I thought you were on limited duty?" I said.

"No such thing around here."

"You think the shooter might try again?"

"I think," Dad pulled out a chair and set his Stetson on the table, "I think that the shooter might try again – and that the person the shooter is trying to get is you."

"Me? You think Charlie Loper has some crazed vendetta against me for organizing his daughter's house?"

"I don't know for sure, darlin', but I'm thinking you need to hand your beauty pageant judgin' to somebody else today."

"Dad, I can't do that. I promised Stan and Rocky."

"Oh, Rocky – the one who just plastered your picture on the front page for the second time in the last week?"

"Okay, I promised Stan," I countered.

"Betsy, you aren't seeing things clearly. Whoever this shooter is, they have two victims now."

"Two people? Are we really classifying Noodles as a human, now?"

"No, we're not." Dad bit his lower lip, making his cop mustache wiggle slightly. "We found Dr. Springer this morning."

I pulled out a chair and joined him at the table. "Where? I didn't hear about this."

"We haven't let the media know about this yet. It's kind of a strange thing, but we might have solved the mystery of the ghost of Charlie Loper."

"You found the ghost?" I stopped to think about this revelation and struggled with a basic fact.

"Shouldn't that person be dead?"

"No, we found Dr. Springer...nearly dead."

"What does that have to do with the ghost of Charlie Loper?"

"We aren't sure yet, except for the fact that we found her dressed up like a cowboy."

This wasn't making any sense. I had seen Dr. Springer right before we started the parade.

"And she was shot? Who shot her?"

"That's the part of the mystery we're still figuring out."

"The last person I saw her talking to was..." I searched my mind. "Clay and Lina Bonnet. They were at the front of the line."

"Okay. Was she dressed like a cowboy then?"

"No," I said. "Why would she dress like Charlie Loper, and why would she be shooting at me?"

"Did you pay your bill on time?"

"Dad," I scolded. Gallows humor was a sure sign of a lifetime cop.

"Where did you find her?"

"She was in the alley behind Earl's Java underneath some black plastic bags. Earl didn't discover her until he took out the trash this morning."

Just another reason to decaffeinate.

"Is she okay?" I asked.

"We can't be sure yet. She lost a lot of blood, but it looks like she made a homemade pressure bandage to try to stop the bleeding."

"Did she say who might have shot her? Did she shoot herself?"

"From the lack of searing or powder burns on her body, we feel she was possibly shot by someone else. We can't be sure who shot her. She wasn't able to talk when we got to her," he said. "Whoever shot her, they left her for dead. I guess she was just like one of those cats she treats and had a few extra lives to trade on. She's in a coma right now."

"So, Dr. Springer was impersonating Charlie Loper and could be our shooter, but we can't question her if she's in a coma and possibly shot by someone else? Do the doctors think she'll come out of it?"

"Maybe," my dad replied. "One thing we figure is that whoever shot her wanted her dead, and for all intents and purposes we are saying she's dead. We have her in the hospital under another name. So if all of this is true, I need you to be out of danger. Is there any way you could cancel all of your public appearances for the few weeks?"

"'If' is the word I'm going to focus on in that sentence," I said. "So let me counter you with an 'if.' If I promise to be vigilant, safe and observant, will you lighten up?"

"Do I have a choice?"

"No."

We heard little feet shuffling into the kitchen. Zach was standing there with his slingshot in his hand. "Don't worry, grandpa. I'll protect Mom. I can get a shot off from pretty far these days."

"Yeah, well, it's just lucky for us all that even though I'm under investigation, Chief Wilson has agreed to let me be out there with my gun and my badge today."

"So do you think he's starting to realize that Bonnet's charge is false?"

"The only thing I've heard lately is that the Bonnets seem to have something else to share with Mr. Cole," he said. "There's some sort of additional evidence now."

"Well, I've been looking through all the pictures I turned in and can't see anything else that could be interpreted as planting evidence," I said with my hand across my heart.

"No, it's something weird. Did you know that the Bonnet farm used to be a ranch run by Charlie Loper?"

Now that was amazing. "No, when did they buy it?"

"That's the thing. They didn't. They've been renting it for the last ten years. At least that's what Clay told the chief."

"So who were they paying rent to? Hunter Grayson?"

"I guess so. I suppose Libby is handling it now," he said. "I don't like the idea of her having to go out there and collect rent from those people."

I envisioned their Rottweiler growling at her when she tried to collect rent. She would do well to get rid of them as tenants.

"If I had to put money on this, as of yesterday I would have pointed at the Bonnets to be Ghost Charlie. Now with Dr. Springer found dressed up like him, I don't know what to think."

"Did she have a gun on her?" I asked.

"Nope, and Art Rivera didn't see any powder burns on her hands. She might have been dressed like Charlie Loper, but she hadn't shot a gun."

"Maybe Dr. Springer was a decoy," I said.

"Could be. And if she was, the shooter is still out there."

"Shooting most of the time near me. I would say at me, but it's always near me."

"Maybe someone is trying to scare you," said my father.

"They've accomplished that," I admitted. "I wish they'd move on to something else on their list."

"Darlin', I would like for you to wear something today."

He rose from the table and went out the back door with a squeak and a slam. He returned momentarily, carrying a white vest connected together with Velcro.

"This here is a covert Kevlar bulletproof vest. You can wear it under your blouse and no one will know the difference."

"Dad! Do you know how hot is out there today? It's the freakin' Fourth of July! I'll die of heatstroke."

"Yeah, well at least we can treat that better than a bullet wound," he said.

"Mom, you need to wear this." Zach put his hands together, pleading. "Please."

I had planned on wearing a white tank top with blue shorts today. Now I'd have to wear something to cover this monstrosity.

"Okay, okay. I'll wear the darn thing. But you'd better be running large cups of sweet tea my way every fifteen minutes."

*****

After Dad left, I had the rest of morning to get ready for the pageant. I was scheduled to be there at 12:30 and planned to enjoy being cool before I had to put on the heavy vest my father had left for me.

I decided to try to call Fitzpatrick one more time. If he had checked out the paper on the Internet today, I had to make it clear to him that I had no interest in Adam Cole. This was probably better than an email, and now I would tell him everything. As I rehearsed in my mind what I would say, I realized something a little bit scary. This was more important to me than I had thought.

The phone rang on the other end, two and then three times.

"Hello." His tone was abrupt.

"Leo? Is that you?"

"Yes."

"Leo, I just wanted to say to you that..."

"Betsy, this isn't necessary. I understand."

"But it is necessary. You need to know that I was never involved..."

"Betsy. I saw your picture. Twice."

"You did?"

"Sure. Your latest escapade was caught in the Pecan Bayou Gazette online today, and while I have to say I'm extremely upset you've been shot at again, I was also not pleased to see you standing with Cole."

Darn that Pecan Bayou Gazette online. Just another reason to take Rocky off my Christmas list.

"No, you don't understand. Adam had just walked up to me and..."

He stopped me cold. "Betsy."

"Yes?"

"Are you all right?"

I was quiet for a moment. I felt my insides melt. Maybe he was going to forgive me. It felt so good.

"Yes," my voice quavered.

"Good. Bye."

With that, the phone clicked silent. Was he saying "good you're not hit," or good as in "goodbye"? I tried a redial, but he didn't pick up. That was it. He was out of my life. My weatherman blew in like a hurricane, and now all I had to do was call the insurance guy and calculate the damage. How could I have been so stupid as to have let this happen?

I slammed my fist down on my desk, sending the printed photos from the Bonnet farm to the floor. I had just lost Leo. I lost him because I was trying to play spy/seductress. Which I also failed at miserably. I felt the tears rushing up as I bent down to pick up the papers, now strewn across the floor of my office. I was so stupid. As I picked up the pictures I had taken of the shed, I leaned up against the desk and sat cross-legged on the floor. When my tears were spent, I sat quietly, the picture still in hand. The color blue caught my eye.

My father was being framed, and now I had proof.

My dad had insisted on George taking us over in the squad car. As soon as we got to the pageant, I would try to tell him.

Chapter 24

"Are you okay?" Stan said, leaning over me as I sat at the judge's table.

"I'm fine. Why do you ask?"

"Your face is terribly red," he said. "Why don't you take off that jacket? It's hotter than blazes out here."

It was pretty hot under the jacket, too. "No, Stan. I'm fine." After viewing my lumpy self with the vest on under a cotton blouse, I decided to take Tory's advice and dress up a little for the pageant. Now I had a choice – look lumpy or sweat like a farmhand in August.

Zach ran up with a large paper cup full of sweet tea. I downed it while he stood there and sent him off for another. I felt my internal temperature recede slightly. I was able to stay a little cooler, but the part I hadn't planned on was the sudden urge to dash to the port-a-potty. I was situated at the front of a long runway, right in the middle of the crowd. Luckily, near the side of the stage area was a row of three port-a-potties. I would be so glad when this day would be over and I could relax in a cool tub.

I could hear the overhead speaker blaring as the announcer invited the crowd: "Y'all come and set a spell for the very first Miss Watermelon contest." Now I realized I had less time than I thought and hurried inside a port-a-potty that stood in a line of the portable outhouses. With the vest hugging me tightly and the closed-in, foul-smelling air of the outdoor toilet, I felt my lunch threatening to come up. I used the bathroom and hurriedly pulled my clothes together and grabbed for the handle of the door. It would not open. I pushed at it with my shoulder, but it still wouldn't budge.

The door of the port-a-potty was jammed. I started slamming my fist against the door and yelling from my blue molded-plastic coffin. Outside I could hear the announcer still calling for the audience to sit down. How long would it be before they noticed one of the judges wasn't there?

I continued to pound on the door, hoping maybe somebody else had to use the bathroom and was waiting outside for the port-a-potty to be available. I put my hands on either side and tried rocking the entire structure. I only made it move slightly as I pushed each side. It started to waver, and I heard the slosh of the disinfectant below the seat. Someone had to be noticing the outhouse rocking out there. The sweat ran down the back of my neck into my snug bulletproof nightmare of a corset. I had to get out before I collapsed from heatstroke. I put all of my energy into one last terrifically hard push. This was it – all or nothing.

I rammed my shoulder up against the door, expecting the thud of the plastic hitting the ground, but instead I felt a whoosh of cool fresh air and a bright light in my eyes.

"Betsy? Damn, get some water, somebody!" I looked up into the blue eyes of my favorite weatherman. Leo Fitzpatrick was here, and he was holding on to little old me.

*****

It was a few minutes later before I was finally able to talk. "The door jammed. I thought I was going to die a disgusting stinky death in there." I gulped down a cup of cool water.

"What do you have on?" Leo asked, feeling my sides, oblivious to the crowd of beauty pageant participants around us.

I squirmed from his touch. "It's a bulletproof vest."

A man broke through the crowd. "Betsy? Did someone shoot at you again?" It was Adam, the one guy I least wanted to have to talk to while being held by Leo.

"No, the door jammed on the port-a-potty."

"That's where you're wrong," said Leo. "When you burst through, a stick went flying in the air. Someone locked you into that thing." Leo stiffened and sat me upright, taking his hands out from under my arms.

"Now that your new boyfriend is here, I'll just be on my way. I left Tyler with Zach, and they're probably lost by now."

"Leo!" I said as he rose and started off. "Leo, wait. You came all this way."

He turned. "Yes, I did. Deep down inside I had to make sure that you and..." he searched for Adam's name, but couldn't quite seem to get it, "...this guy were an item. My suspicions have been confirmed."

"Leo!" I had to make him understand.

A woman came running up behind Adam Cole and grabbed hold of his waist. "I found you! I didn't think I'd ever get finished at the department." He turned to Elena Morris and kissed her. I couldn't believe it. Elena and Adam? That fast? I sat on the pavement, stunned.

Adam looked down at me and extended his free hand to help me up. He turned to Leo, "You were saying what about me and Betsy?"

Leo's jaw slackened. His pace had been going in the other direction, but now he turned and grabbed me up from the pavement by my other arm. "Come with me," he said.

"Leo, I can't go with you, I have to go judge a beauty pageant in about five minutes."

"Five minutes is all I'll need."

Stan stepped in front us, stopping Leo's momentum. "It's just going to have to wait, loverboy." Stan's nose curled up. "Betsy, do you have any perfume in your bag? You smell awful."

"Sorry," I said. I turned to Leo. "Please, there about twenty little girls and twenty soon-to-be angry family members over there waiting for me. I need to go."

He relented. "Go," was his one-word answer. Somehow I worried that my going meant more than go judge a beauty pageant. Was he releasing me out of whatever it was we had? I had to admit he had been more than patient with me, but the thought of him out of my life left a sadness deep inside of me.

I walked over to the judging table and pulled out my purse to spray on some perfume. After a quick search, I surmised that all I had was hand sanitizer. I spread the clear goo over my hands, face and neck and tried to make it a little shower in a bottle. At least the alcohol in the gel made it cool on my skin. A lady sitting nearby smiled and scooted a few inches away. Let the judging begin.

Stan ran up. "Okay, Betsy, here are your ballots to score each little Miss Watermelon contestant."

Rocky came up behind him with his camera around his neck. "We're using a full-color picture on the front, so a nice red, white and blue dress would be great. Oh, and no goofy kids."

"All kids are goofy, don't you know that?" I said, pulling the ballot sheets in front of me. Rocky sat on the edge of my table and leaned over.

"What's that smell? It's kind of a mixture of sewer water and Lysol." I elbowed him off the table as Stan rose to the platform to start the proceedings.

"I'm here! Am I late?" Tory came running in and pulled out her chair. A diamond tiara about blinded me as the sun bounced off its rhinestones. She also had on a midnight blue evening gown and a sash that read "Miss Hill Country 1995." She noted my shock and continued, "I am a former pageant winner. It's good for the girls to see that winning a pageant is a lifelong commitment."

I wasn't sure if that was a good thing or a bad thing.

Behind us we had the official crew of NUTV – one camera man and one sound man. These guys had a lot of experience, but mostly from shooting high school football and the farm and ranch report. I turned around to wave at them, and the microphone guy was biting into a footlong hot dog. He nodded his head in acknowledgement. I turned back as strains of orchestra music started through the speakers.

"Ladies and gentlemen, we are proud to present our beautiful girls in the very first Pecan Bayou Miss Watermelon Pageant. Let's give them all a hand!" Stan said, dressed in yellow slacks and a blue-and-white striped shirt. If I had to guess, it was probably Ralph Lauren he had on today.

The smallest girls came out first, one by one turning in their red, white and blue dresses. One little girl came toward me with hair sprayed into a style that was so much larger than her head I worried about the weight on her neck. She sashayed toward me, ruffling a petticoat under a white satin skirt. She had on more bling than one of Donald Trump's wives. Out in the audience I heard a woman yell, "Sparkle, baby!" and the little girl smiled even wider.

As the sun caught her bedazzled rhinestones, it reminded me of something. Each time the ghost of Charlie Loper shot, I saw something sparkling in the light. Either Charlie Loper was a showgirl in the afterlife or the killer had on something that would catch the light. I had to concentrate on the next contestant and the next and the next. I would worry about the killer later, after the pageant.

There was only one problem – they were all cute. Not a dog in the bunch. Lots of hairspray, lots of lipgloss and hundreds of dollars worth of silk and taffeta. Maybe a more experienced judge would know what to count off on. I noticed Tory busily scratching out commentaries on each and every girl. Her judging sheets would be worthy of framing by the time she was finished with them. I looked at the criteria on the judging sheets – personality, poise, appropriate outfit – they all had that. As the last one walked through, I knew I was in big trouble. I had to do something to pick just one. There was a tiara under a glass case on the side of the stage, and I knew that I couldn't give it to all of them.

My dad stood to the side of the crowd, quietly speaking into his shoulder walkie. I felt like the president surrounded by Secret Service agents. What was their code name for me? The Hopeless Hinter? Could there really be someone out here who wanted to do me harm?

I was surprised to see Coop Bonnet, leaning up against the Bonnet Farm watermelon booth, observing the pageant. Too hot for the leather jacket, today he had on a red muscle shirt and mirrored sunglasses. His head turned slightly in my direction. I quickly averted my gaze. Was he lining up his next shot? I wonder if he had jammed any sticks in port-a-potty doors lately. I started writing on one of my scoring sheets, trying to look busy. Tory looked over and smiled. Maybe I was finally doing it right.

Stan got up to announce the sportswear competition, and like clockwork the littlest ones came out first. They were in red, white and blue shorts and summer dresses and looked a little more comfortable carrying their giant heads of hair down the runway. All of the girls paraded through again. I wrote down descriptions of the girls and things I liked on the ballots and once again, knew I was stumped. This was like trying to pick a favorite child. Over in the first few rows I could see parents craning their necks to watch both their children and the reactions on the judges' faces at the same time. As the last contestant entered the backstage area, Stan announced a ten-minute break while the judges tallied up their score sheets.

Tory pulled a little rhinestone-studded calculator out of her purse and started furiously punching in numbers with her red lacquered nails. I continued on with my trusty pencil and started adding up my own numbers. As I finished I had to come to a decision. If I turned in my sheets as-is, then the person who would decide the first Miss Watermelon would be Tory. This didn't seem like a bad idea, but I just needed something else. All of these girls and their parents were professionals at the presentation side of things, but really what was this pageant named for? Watermelons.

"The judges look like they might be ready to turn in their score sheets, ladies and gentlemen," Stan said, showing off his freshly whitened smile. I timidly raised my hand.

"Uh, Stan. I was wondering if I could ask a question of the contestants?"

Stan continued smiling, but his eyes spoke a different language. I had just gone off the script.

"That was Betsy Livingston, ladies and gentlemen, our helpful hints columnist from the newspaper." He emphasized "helpful hints" as in, "What the hell does she know?"

"She would like to ask a question of our beautiful young ladies." With that, the parents turned to each other and started violently whispering. Questions were not listed on the requirements, and there was going to be trouble. Lord knows that if they had known, they would have drilled their kids like the night before the SAT.

"What are you doing?" Tory whispered.

"I just need ... something more."

"No, you don't."

"Yes, I do." I stood up. "Because this is a pageant for Miss Watermelon, I was just wondering if any of the girls could tell me the nutritional value of a watermelon."

A hush fell over the crowd. The girls on the stage dropped their smiles one by one, some of them licking their dried-out teeth. I heard Stan clear his throat. What had I just done?

One little girl pushed through the crowd. I recognized her as the now-grieving owner of Noodles the dead poodle, Nora Nicholson.

"Although high in sugar, watermelon is very low in saturated fat, cholesterol and sodium. It is also a good source of potassium, vitamin A and vitamin C." She stepped back and then forward again and said, "Thank you," and stepped back again.

Her mother yelled out, "Excellent work, Nora!"

"Indeed!" said Stan, his smile back in place. "What a beautiful, talented and smart group of girls we have here today. Does that suffice, Mrs. Livingston?"

"I think that will do just fine," I answered, sitting back down. I quickly scribbled a few things down and noticed Tory adding something to her score sheets. We simultaneously handed them over to

Stan. "I will tally the judges' scores while our lovely young ladies take one more spin down the runway," he said.

The orchestra music came back over the loudspeakers, and I heaved a sigh of relief. No matter how much Rocky and Stan might beg me, I would never ever judge a beauty pageant again.

"Good question, darlin'," my dad said from behind me, putting his hand on my shoulder.

"You are full of surprises, Betsy," said Tory, sitting up straight in her chair.

"And you're good at judging beauty, Tory. I just felt totally inadequate at the job. I hope I didn't mess things up."

"On the contrary. I've been judging beauty pageants in this area for the last twenty years, and I can tell you I have never heard anyone shut the parents up before. That little girl showed true grace under pressure, a quality every beauty queen must have. Good job."

I was amazed I had done something right. I looked over at Leo sitting with Tyler and Zach. They all gave me a thumbs-up.

"Where's Aunt Maggie and Danny?" I asked, looking around.

"Danny isn't doing too good after the parade yesterday. He had trouble sleeping and kept telling Maggie he saw Charlie Loper. They're spending the day at home, watching High School Hijinks on the television and staying cool. They're going to try and make it to the fireworks tonight."

Had I become so desensitized to being shot at that I didn't even think about the effect it would have on Danny? When things really scared him, he could just shut down. He didn't understand everything that was going on, so rather than try he would take himself out of the picture. After my uncle died, he didn't want to go to the funeral. We left him with a friend and his parents, and they played video games while we buried his father.

"I'm so sorry to hear that. We'll stop by on the way home and bring him a hot dog and some cotton candy," I said. "Oh, and I need to talk with you about something. Something I figured out from the pictures."

"From what pictures?" he asked, but then Stan returned to the stage holding a white card. "Okay, Pecanites. We have a winner of the Miss Watermelon crown." Stan looked over at the gathering of nervous little girls. "And the winner is...Nora..." From behind us, the sound of a soulful cowboy song was coming out of the loudspeakers, overtaking Stan's announcement. It was eerie-sounding – and then a voice spoke though the undertones of a guitar strum.

"Howdy, buckaroos and buckarettes. This is your old pal Charlie Loper. I don't think some of you've been livin' the cowboy way." Sparks started shooting out of the port-a-potty I had been trapped in. With a giant explosion, its blue plastic door blasted off its hinges and flew right toward us. I crawled under the judges' table with Tory Parker.

As soon as the door landed, the structure stood on its side, altered by the explosion. Luckily there didn't seem to be any inhabitants at the time of the blast.

Dad rushed out from under the table just as the crowd started pulling themselves out from under their folding metal chairs. Leo came running toward me with Zach and Tyler running along behind.

"Betsy!" he yelled. "Where are you?" I crawled out from the under the tablecloth, red garland strewn in my hair.

"Hiding under here in the flying outhouse safe zone," I said.

Leo reached down and helped me up. "Thank God. What is it with you and port-a-potties today?"

"Yeah, well, this time I don't think it was just me. It was the ghost of Charlie Loper, taking vengeance on the entire town."

"No, Betsy. Either you're really unlucky, or someone is after you. Look at the facts, you've been shot at twice, and now ..."

"The would-be victim of a port-a-potty explosion," I said dryly. I was coming to the creeping conclusion that I had been face-to-face with the killer some time in the last weeks and let something slip.

Libby Loper ran up onto the stage, today dressed in a white top and jean skirt with white boots. She tipped back her Stetson and picked up the microphone.

"Is this thing on?" she said, making half the crowd cover their ears. "Sorry, but I just needed to say something to whoever this is playing like they are my dear departed father. It's all lies. My father was a good man and would never, ever harm a single soul. When they catch this person, I will be suing them for slander. They are ruining his reputation and breaking my heart." Libby put the microphone back and slowly walked off the stage. I reached out for her as she passed by.

"Are you okay?" I asked.

She just nodded her head in disgust and walked back into the crowd.

"Wow, that was so cool," Zach said, pointing to the bent plastic port-a-potty door now lying next to the runway.

My dad walked up with police from Andersonville on each side of him. "Leo, could you get my daughter out of here?"

"Dad! I am standing right here, and I can get myself home, thank you."

"Leo?" my dad, repeated issuing a command this time. Leo took a protective hold under my arm, and I barely grabbed my purse as we exited the fairgrounds.

"Wait! I wanted to get Danny some cotton candy," I said, pulling free.

"Oh, all right, just because it's for Danny," said Leo. I went to the window of the cotton candy trailer and ordered a blue one for my cousin. After Zach and Tyler noticed what I was doing, I ordered a couple more.

I hadn't gotten a chance to talk to my dad about what I had figured out from the pictures. I had to make some time to either talk to him or to go back out and see if I could find what I thought I was seeing.

"Ready?" said Leo.

"Yes," I answered. "If we could just run this by Aunt Maggie's on the way home before it melts, it would really help Danny. He got pretty shook up from the shooting yesterday."

Zach spoke over his blue cotton candy, his face now starting to resemble Papa Smurf. "Did you know a poodle was shot dead, right in the middle of Main Street? You should have seen it."

We all piled into Leo's SUV. He turned the key and then turned to me and cocked his head. "Betsy? How do you get into all these messes? It's absolutely risky to care for a person who is constantly getting shot at or locked in a port-a-potty. Is your life ever boring?"

"My life is just like anyone else's, it's just it's been a little hectic this week."

"Little more than hectic."

"Well, you didn't have to come down here. You could have just stayed in Dallas," I snapped.

That set the tone in the car, and not in a good way. I felt a pounding headache coming on, probably from sitting in the heat wearing an extra twenty pounds and nearly dying in the port-a-potty. I stripped off the jacket and started unbuttoning my blouse to pull off the bulletproof vest.

Leo looked over and then spoke to the boys. "Close your eyes, boys."

I looked over to see both boys with their eyes covered.

"Take that thing off. No wonder you're so hot."

I pulled off the Velcro fasteners and felt the rush of air conditioning hit my exposed skin. I sighed and then looked over to see Leo, barely watching the road. He swerved slightly.

"Uh, sorry."

I smiled and buttoned up my blouse again. When we got to Aunt Maggie's, Leo volunteered to run in the cotton candy and we then we headed for home.

"Do you feel okay? You're starting to look pale," he said.

"I'm fine, just need an ibuprofen," I yawned.

"And maybe a nap," Leo said, the trace of a smile playing on his lips.

"Mom, you can't have a headache. We have to go to the fireworks tonight!" In all the excitement, I had forgotten that the Fourth of July was one of those days that can last into eternity.

"Tell you what," Leo said as we walked into the house, "you take a nap and the boys and I will figure out something to eat. How does that sound?"

"Sounds great," I said, yawning.

After taking an ibuprofen with a cold glass of water I shut my eyes and tried to get all the scenes from the last week from playing in mind. Hunter Grayson's body kept flashing in along with the vibrant blue of the inside of the port-a-potty. Charlie Loper kept appearing on the balcony and then disappearing. Butch kept running away, ready to navigate to streets of Pecan Bayou. My cell phone rang in my purse by the bed. I rummaged around for it, and Rocky Whitson's number shone across the electric screen.

"Yo, Betsy. I'm heading back to the office. Got some fine shots of the blown-up outhouse. I hate to be asking this of you, but with all that happened today, I didn't get a picture of you and Miss Watermelon. Could you possibly come down to the Gazette for a quick photo op? I've already lined up Miss Watermelon and her mother."

"Rocky, really? You haven't exactly done me too many favors lately."

"Betsy, I also may hae something more on your dad's investigation." Rocky said.

"I'm on my way." I said as I hung up the phone. I yawned as the smell of cooking hamburger drifted to me from the kitchen. I slipped on my shoes and ran a brush through my hair and stepped out to find the boys demolishing enormous cheese burgers. Butch waited patiently by the table for any scraps that might fall his way.

"You're up! Have a nice nap?"

"Much better."

Leo pulled a plate out of the cupboard to make me a burger.

"Looks wonderful. Could you wrap it up for me? Rocky needs me at the paper for a picture. If you could take the boys to the fireworks, I'll meet you there."

"Are you sure that's such a good idea? Just tell him no."

"I tried that but he says he has information on my dad." Leo handed me sandwich in a paper towel. I took a bite and headed out to my car.

Chapter 25

Ten minutes later as I smiled for the camera with Pecan Bayou's newest Miss Watermelon, I had to wonder what Rocky had up his sleeve. He had lured me down here on the premise of something new in my father's investigation, but waiting out the picture session felt like an eternity.

"Well, ladies. That ought to do it," he said finally.

Mellie Nicholson took little Nora by the shoulders and reached out and shook my hand. "I just want to thank you for your in-depth questioning. Without it, we never would have had a chance. This week has been so dramatic for us, what with Noodle's being gunned down in the street and now this. I can remember a poem from my English class years ago. I think it was Cheney who said, 'The soul would have no rainbow had the eyes no tears.' We have certainly experienced the rainbow today."

"I'm just glad it's all over," Nora said.

"Nora!"

"Well, Grandma, you have to admit this whole pageant thing is a lot of work."

"Yes, but it's a labor of love, right, sweetheart?"

Nora shifted on one foot and then shot a glance at her grandmother. "If you say so. When are you going to get another dog?"

Mrs. Nicholson reached down and put her arms around Nora. "As soon as the kennel opens. I think you've earned it."

"Thanks again," she said, and the two finally exited.

"Who'd have thought Mrs. Nicholson would know poetry?" Rocky laughed.

"Hey, lots of people have a hidden cultural side. You can never tell," I said, remembering the book of poems Hunter Grayson had penned. I had forgotten to give the little journal to my dad.

"So what have you found out about my dad's case?"

"You get straight to the point Betsy, and that's why I love editing your work. It's like a vacation for me."

"Thank you, I try my best."

"Rocky went to his desk at the back of the room and pulled up a screen on his computer. "Did you know that Libby Loper owns the Bonnet Farm?"

"Old news, Rocky. I know and the police know."

"Did you know that Charlie Loper is buried out there?"

"That's not what I heard," I said. "I was always told he was buried out in California with all the other dead movie cowboys."

"That's what they told everyone, but really there's just a headstone in California," Rocky said. "Charlie is buried out in the trees beyond the fields. I guess the old boy got uncomfortable around crowds, so his final wishes were to be buried on his ranch."

"Land, lots of land under starry skies above, right?" I said. "So how does all this help my dad?"

"It doesn't, but I did hear that Libby Loper went out to the farm to check out the property and they were not exactly welcoming to her. She wanted to walk the property line and visit her dad's grave, and they wouldn't allow it. Now Libby is threatening to evict them."

"Okay, and how does this exactly help my dad?"

"Don't you see? They have something to hide out there. If Libby does get out there and discovers something, then it could make your dad's case look like a yelping dog complaint. Whatever they're doing out there, it's big."

"I have a pretty good idea, although I'm not sure exactly where. Hunter Grayson had a bag of pot in his pocket. A bag with a piece of blue plastic in it. I had seen that blue plastic one other place."

Rocky's police scanner went off in the background. "10-51. Loper vehicle, tires slashed." George's voice said over the static-filled airwaves.

"Looks like the battle goes on, Betsy. How much you wanna bet the Bonnets' slashed her tires?" Rocky grabbed his keys and his camera and started for the door. "Lock the door on your way out."

Chapter 26

As the sun slowly set in the Texas heat, I made my way to the fireworks. My time at Rocky's office had made me late to meet Leo and the boys. I pulled into the field that served as a parking lot, which was nearly full already. I realized I had never brought the box from Libby Loper's house out of my car. The book of Hunter's poetry was still perched at the top of the heap. I thought about putting the journal in my purse but found it wouldn't fit. I didn't want to carry it around all night, so I would try to pull Dad over tonight and talk to him.

Leo also said he wanted to talk to me. I just hoped that he wasn't about to tell me it was over between us. If he could just understand that it all started with the dog and trying to keep my son happy. From there we had a murder, and from there somebody shooting pistols but never hitting anything but a dog. Surely he'd had other girlfriends who had found themselves in trouble from time to time.

I walked over to the field, where I found Leo spreading a blanket on the ground. The boys collapsed onto it as soon as it hit the grass.

"Look at the stars, Zach. I think I can see the Big Dipper."

"That's Scorpio, boys. Can't you see its distinctive tail?" Leo corrected.

The joys of hanging out with a meteorologist. Leo outlined the shape of a scorpion with his finger as both boys emitted an appreciative "cool." He smiled, making the little crows feet appear around his eyes. Why did men look handsome and distinguished with that kind of thing and women just looked tired? Zach struggled with a juice box, and Leo still gazing at the stars, put his hand out for it and inserted the flimsy straw into the top. No doubt about it, this was quite a guy.

He suddenly looked over, aware of my surveillance and tilted his eyes to the side. "The stars are usually further up than that, Betsy."

Smartass. "I knew that." So why did this guy have to be so darn frustrating?

"Betsy, let's sit over here." He pointed to the remainder of the blanket left from the boys stretching out to look at the stars. "We need to talk."

Oh boy, this couldn't be good. Don't people start a breakup with those kinds of words?

I scooted onto the blanket, and he pulled me in next to him. Well, this couldn't be too bad, I thought as I felt his arms go around and I leaned back in perfect comfort. This was better than any La-Z-Boy recliner I'd ever sat in. I sighed and felt myself relaxing. I could always be mad at him tomorrow.

"So, I was thinking the other night."

"Good."

"About us and this uh, rough patch we've been going through."

Uh oh, here it came.

"Betsy!" Danny came stumbling onto the blanket, nearly knocking Leo and me over. "Fireworks, Betsy! Where's Butch?"

"We left him home so he could crawl under the bed. He's probably not going to like the fireworks." Leo said.

"Oh my, I'm sorry, you two." Aunt Maggie was power-walking behind Danny, but he had outdistanced her. She was holding a brown plaid blanket and a small cooler. "Danny's pretty excited."

Leo laughed. "I can see that."

Behind Maggie stood the tall, gangly Howard Gunther, the leader of the official Pecan Bayou Paranormal Society. He carried a black duffle bag in one hand and used his other hand to smooth back his thin white hair.

"Good evening, all." Howard bowed.

"Howard! I haven't seen you in while. How's the world of ghosts?" Leo said.

Howard snorted. "If you are referring to my study of the paranormal, then I must tell you it's fine."

I nudged Aunt Maggie and whispered, "Is Howard your date?"

Her hand went to her ample bosom, "Oh, no my dear." She giggled. "Howard is here in case we have a sighting of Charlie Loper. He ought to be able to authenticate any apparition we might encounter."

I could do without a sighting of Charlie Loper, seeing as every time he showed up, he seemed to be shooting at me. I glanced across the crowd, now starting to settle down for the fireworks. Little Miss Watermelon sat in a customized lawn chair wearing her rhinestone-studded tiara and eating a Fudgsicle. Libby Loper had also found her way here, even with slashed tires. She was sitting with Ruby Green and a few of the other Hair House ladies, leaning up against the biggest drink cooler on the ground. A few blankets over, Ruby's brother, Pastor Green, shot her a disapproving look as she laughed and popped the top on a Lone Star beer and waved him off. He smiled and walked over for a can, much to the dismay of his wife.

Farther up the field were Clay and Lina Bonnet. Clay sat upright, looking like he had better places to go. Lina poured him some soda out of a two-liter bottle, which he took begrudgingly. Next to them, Adam Cole sat alone. I hoped he wouldn't come over. Leo had his arms around me, and I would hate to mess that up now. Cole started to rise, but then Elena came over and set down a plate of nachos. Adam's gaze rose to her and then seemed to skirt across the sea of blankets to me. I quickly looked away, embarrassed at seeing this intimate moment. He probably thought I was pining for him to come join me on my blanket. I was pretty happy on my blanket with two preteen boys stretched out on it and me luxuriating against Leo's warm chest.

Allison walked by on the edge of the crowd. She was with another young woman whose arm was linked with hers. At a time like this, it was good she had a friend. The attempted murder of Dr. Springer was awful, and the fact that she was found dressed up like Charlie Loper didn't help matters any. Had Jean Springer been masquerading as the ghost of Charlie Loper? If so, why? What was in it for her? The two girls walked by, and Allison waved at our group gathered on the blanket. Danny looked up from his snack assortment and waved hard enough to stir up a breeze.

"Hey Danny," she said but didn't linger to talk. I wondered if Allison was avoiding Danny. Luckily, for Danny just saying "hello" was quite enough to make him happy. He beamed at her as she walked away.

Mayor Obermeyer came out in front of the crowd waving a handheld microphone.

"Okay folks, we are about to start our fireworks show here tonight. Before we begin, if I could have everyone stand and place their hands over their hearts to sing our national anthem. We will be accompanied by the summer school session of the Pecan Bayou High School marching band. Seeing as it's fairly dark, though, they won't be marching tonight," he reassured us.

We all scrambled to our feet as I heard a slightly flat clarinet play a note to tune the band. When the band was ready, we all joined in like we always had before basketball, football and baseball games in this town. Zach and Tyler were standing between me and Leo, mouthing the words of the song, the pureness of patriotism flowing while they jabbed each other with their elbows. I leaned over to tell Zach to cut it out when I was pushed into them by someone rushing through the crowd. The smell of cheap aftershave filled my nostrils.

"Out of my way, bitch." Coop Bonnet slunk off into the people still singing along.

"He's not going to get away with that," Leo said, starting off after him.

"No, it's okay." I placed my hand on his arm. "He's just angry about my dad arresting him.

"Yeah, well, he doesn't need to treat you that way."

"I said it's okay." Leo huffed and stepped back beside me, moving the boys over. He placed his arm protectively around my waist, and again I felt comfortable almost as if I had been standing in the embrace of this man for my entire life.

From about forty feet away, I saw a familiar sparkle. Lights on the park gazebo were catching the light of something. It was happening again.

"Get down!" I shouted. No one could hear me over the group singing. "Get down!" I pulled Leo and the boys down to the blanket, making everyone around us stop singing.

"Gun!" I yelled.

Screams rang out, and people everywhere started picking up their blankets and coolers and running for the trees.

"It's the ghost of Charlie Loper!" Mr. Simmons cried out.

"Oh hell," I heard my father say. We picked up our various belongings, and as I glanced over I could see Danny trying to put each and every item he had so painstakingly set out back into the cooler. Aunt Maggie was pulling at him trying to get him to move. Howard must have already run for cover. Leo and I exchanged glances. He grabbed the boys and I made my way through the crowd to Danny's blanket.

"Come on, Danny. We have to go," I said.

"We can't go. The fireworks haven't happened."

"I know, but we have to go." The field was almost completely cleared. There was only one thing missing. Where was the shooter? I had never actually seen a gun, just the sparkle that always came right before it. Had I reacted to something as silly as an errant firefly or someone's glow-in-the-dark wand? I noticed people standing on the edges of the field looking out at me with the same question playing across their faces. I had thrown a panic, and the bad guy never showed up. It was the equivalent to yelling "Fire!" in a crowded theater.

Coop Bonnet emerged from the edge of the crowd and walked toward Danny. I wasn't sure if he was there to help or to just beat the living tar out of him. "Come on, Danny. Let's go over here for a minute before the fireworks. Okay?"

Danny pushed his glasses up on his nose. He reached up for Coop. "Okay," he agreed, letting himself be pulled up by the hand. He still held on tight to his box of Rice Krispie treats with the other hand. They started walking toward the crowd, where a faint clap went up. Coop put his arm around Danny and talked to him in a whisper. Danny kept nodding his head and then smiled at him. Maybe Coop wasn't all that bad. I didn't even know he knew Danny.

Then it was quiet as the crowd looked around for the ghostly appearance of Charlie. The quiet continued, but still nothing happened. I had been wrong.

"Betsy!" I turned around and saw my dad standing there, a vein throbbing in his forehead. "Why in the hell would you yell 'gun' in the middle of a crowd of people?"

"I thought I saw one." I returned to Danny who was looking up at Coop and smiling. "I saw the sparkle." I said feeling foolish.

Dad started to speak and then stopped himself. I could tell he was mentally trying to pull it together rather than what doing he really wanted to do.

"A sparkle? You cleared a crowd because you saw a sparkle?"

"Dad, you have to understand. Each time before the gun went off I saw something sparkling, followed by a cloud of smoke."

"It was the ghost of Charlie Loper!" Mr. Simmons yelled from the edge of the field. The crowd nodded in agreement.

Howard stepped out, holding up a small recording device.

"Charlie? Are you here Charlie? Do you have something to tell us?" He paused between each sentence so that Charlie could have time to speak from another plane of existence.

"Dammit! You people are crazy. I was better off on drugs!" Libby Loper stepped out from the crowd. "My daddy is not back from the dead, and if he was, he sure as hell was a better shot than the one that's shooting at you idiots."

"It's the sparkle," continued Mr. Simmons. "Don't you know, your daddy wore them sparkly-looking chaps and vests. He walked into my store back in '57, and I darn near had to turn the overhead lights down, he was glitterin' so." His audience was visibly entertained.

"You see what you've started," Dad said. He raised his hands to the crowd. "Folks, we've been through quite a bit these last few days, so Betsy here might have jumped the gun."

He would have to say that word.

"I don't see any shooters out there, so why don't we just relax and enjoy our fireworks?" he continued.

"I second the motion," Mayor Obermeyer added.

People started back out onto the field, many of them shooting me surly looks. Who knows, I thought. I might have saved somebody's life – or at least some unsuspecting poodle's life.

"Betsy, keep an eye on Danny," said Aunt Maggie. "Howard and I are going to do some investigative work. Just listen to this."

She held up the tiny digital recorder to my ear. I could clearly hear Howard's voice. "Charlie Loper? Can you hear me? Please speak to us." After that, I heard crackly white noise and then an indistinguishable "frmmp."

"Frmmp? What is that?" I said.

"You just don't know how to listen with a practiced ear," said Howard. "It is clear to me that he is saying 'dump.' He wants us to meet him at the dump."

I raised my eyebrows. Charlie Loper is hanging out with the trash and he wants my aunt to meet him there?

"I don't think so, Aunt Maggie. I know I have an unpracticed ear, but I sure didn't pick up 'meet me at the dump,'" I said.

"Nevertheless, we might not get a chance like this again, especially if he chooses to cross into the light. Can Danny stay with you?"

Fireworks started going off behind us.

"Um, sure. No problem. He can come and sit with us on our blanket to watch the fireworks." I glanced around to see him sitting cross-legged on his blanket, now drinking an orange soda.

"No, he said he wanted to sit on our blanket." Aunt Maggie cupped her hand to her mouth and whispered, "He got to pack his own snack, and he's not feeling like sharing tonight."

I smiled. "Gotcha," I said.

I settled back into our blanket, sitting with my knees up to my chin.

"Where's Maggie going?" Leo asked.

"She's off to the dump to have a one-on-one with Charlie Loper."

"The dump? You think he could have picked someplace that smells better than that."

The boys now sat in front of us, echoing the crowd with the obligatory oohs and ahhs that came with each display of pyrotechnics.

"So, you really thought you saw a shooter?" Leo asked placing his hands around my waist. "Hey, where's the bulletproof vest?"

"Shhh, I told my dad I was wearing it tonight. I just couldn't put it back on after the last time. I thought I was going to sweat to death in that thing. Whoever is shooting at me can't seem to hit the side of a barn anyway, so why wear it?"

"Well, I can't complain," Leo said, "but Betsy, I just wish you'd be more careful."

"Leo, nothing's going to happen. You and my dad both need to relax."

Leo's body stiffened. "It's pretty tough when you keep calling me and telling me you've been shot at or you found yet another dead body lying around here in Pecan Bayou, the unofficial murder capital of Texas."

"To be fair, I didn't call you the last couple of times."

"Yeah, that's right. Your picture was all over the Internet. My bad on that one."

"Leo, I don't need you to come down here and be my knight in shining armor. I'm doing just fine. You have enough stuff going on in your own life."

"What are you trying to say?" The boys turned from their sky gazing and uttered a sibilant "Shhh!"

"Sorry," I said in a whisper. "I don't know what I'm trying to say, it's just that I feel..." I glanced over to Danny's blanket. His cooler was there, but he was nowhere near.

"Where's Danny?" I said.

Leo looked back. "He was sitting right there."

"This can't be good," I rose from the blanket.

"Maybe he went to use the men's room," Leo said. "I'll check for him there."

"I'll get my dad looking with the rest of the guys from the police. Boys, you stay here and do *not* move an inch. Do you hear me?" They both looked up at me wide-eyed. "Yes, ma'am."

We split up, going different directions. Leo headed for the outdoor restrooms in the park, and I started looking into the different crowds of people to see if Danny might have joined one of them. If Allison was still around with her friend, he might have wandered over to talk to them. Dad, who had really wanted to take this night off, stood on the edge of the crowd talking with George and pointing up at the sky.

"Dad, we've lost Danny."

"When did you see him last?"

"He was sitting right over there. Aunt Maggie went off with Howard to the dump to talk to Charlie Loper."

My dad sighed and ran his hands through his graying hair. "And this is why my own family causes me more problems than any other family in the city of Pecan Bayou." He put his hand on George's shoulder ready to issue orders.

"George, you start scanning the crowd and see if he joined someone else on their blanket. Get Elena on it, too. I'll check out the cars in the parking lot."

"What about me?" I asked.

"Betsy, you need to get back to your son before I have to go out looking for him, too. I've got enough on my plate without trying to keep you out of danger."

I gulped. "Really? You're sending me back to the blanket?"

"I certainly am."

I trudged back over to the boys, obediently watching three starbursts of red, white and blue.

"You got told to sit here too, huh, Mom?" Zach said, patting my back.

"You heard that?"

"Sure. You might be a mom, but to grandpa you're still his kid."

"I suppose," I said.

"Did they find Danny?" Tyler asked.

"Not yet."

"Maybe he's doing his special favor for his special friend," Zach said, then sucked down the insides of a juice box.

"What special favor?" I asked.

"I don't know. He didn't say."

"Zach, this could be important. Just what did Danny tell you?"

"He said that he had to go and do a special favor for a special friend, and only he could do it."

"Why didn't you say something sooner?"

"I thought you knew."

"How would I know? Is there anything else you would like to tell me?"

"Um, he asked me to lend him your keys. He needed to get something out of your car."

"My car?" I jumped up and turned around, pointing my finger back at the boys. "Don't move!" I demanded.

I ran to my car, now situated between many others parked in the grass. I squeezed into my side of the car and looked to see if Danny was sleeping in the backseat. I turned on the dome light, but the back seat was empty. A few stray papers and a leftover fast food bag were strewn on the floor. The box from Libby's house was still in the front seat. The contents of the box looked like it had been searched through in a hurry. Hunter Grayson's book of poetry was no longer there. Was that what Danny had been after as a favor to his 'special friend'? I noticed a smell in the car that hadn't been there before. It was an overwhelming smell of men's cologne. Who was the special friend anyway? I remembered Coop Bonnet whispering to him just a little while ago. I was touched by his demonstration of caring toward my cousin, but his sudden kindness seemed out of place now.

Chapter 27

I tried to recall if I had heard the bass tones of the muffler on Coop's Corvette. With all of the sounds of the fireworks it could have easily blended in. Glancing back at the boys on the blanket, I searched the crowd. If Danny's life was in danger, he wouldn't even know it until it was too late. I turned back toward the car and in the distance picked up just a tiny red glow across the park. Somebody was over in the gazebo. It had to be Coop. I shut my car door and started sprinting in the dark toward the glowing red light. The closer I got to Coop, the stronger the scent of the repugnant cologne, mixed with cigarette smoke, filled my nose.

"Betsy! Betsy!" I heard Danny's voice clearly through the darkness.

"Betsy, Betsy," Coop said, imitating Danny's speech impediment, his arms flailing at his sides.

"Hi Betsy!" Danny, oblivious to the situation, sounded happy to see me.

Suddenly upon them, I stopped short, gasping for breath. I tried to sound calm. "Hi Danny. Are you and Mr. Coop okay?"

"Yes, Betsy. He's my special friend."

"I see – and is he the one you did the favor for?"

"Yes."

"What did you do?"

"I got the book for him. He likes to read."

I smirked at Coop, now feeling even more than disgust for him. I grabbed Danny by the arm. "Well now he has it, so let's leave him alone to catch up on his reading."

"Cousin Betsy. He can't read in the dark," Danny said.

"That's right," said Coop. "I can't read in the dark, and besides, what's your hurry? You coming over here couldn't have worked out better."

"Are you finally going to try to shoot me and actually hit me?" I said. "Is that it? You've been shooting at me all this time, just for that stupid book?"

Coop grabbed Danny's other arm and yanked him back toward him. Danny struggled to release himself from Coop's hold.

"Let him go." I reached out, attempting to pull his hand off of Danny. Coop dropped the book and backhanded me on the cheek, knocking me to the floor of the gazebo.

"Back off, bitch," he said as I sat on the ground rubbing my jaw.

"Stop it," Danny said. "Betsy, I want to go home now."

I rose again and plowed into Coop headlong.

"Enough!" A female voice came out of the darkness just as Coop's rebuff of my force landed me back on the ground.

From out of the shadows, Allison Emory stepped into the light. "Man, Betsy – you don't give up, do you?" She picked up Hunter Grayson's notebook from the ground. In her other hand was a glistening golden Colt revolver pointed directly at me.

She gestured to Danny with the gun. "Let him go, Coop."

Coop complied and pushed Danny toward me. I stood up and put my arm around his trembling shoulders.

"Thank you, Allison. You keep him here, and I'll go get the police." I turned with Danny to go but noticed that Allison had put her arms around Coop and was pulling his head down to kiss him on the lips. She pulled back from their embrace, and a slow grin spread across her face. The golden Colt was again pointed directly at me.

"Your father messed everything up for us, you know," she said. "Him and his badass cop routine. He thought he was so cool because he found a little pot on Coop. Ooh-wee, big narcotics haul in the city of Pecan Bayou. Your old man didn't know the half of it."

"I guess he didn't," I replied. "However, I was starting to figure it out."

"What do you know?" Coop said.

"I know that if I were to take a really close look at that shed out at the farm, I'd find a whole lot more than watermelons. I'm guessing you and your father have quite a successful farm, both legally and illegally. That's why the Bonnets only let people in certain sections. It's also why they won't let Libby Loper visit her father's grave."

"Just where would we be doing this? Between the watermelons and the grapes?" Coop snorted, laughing at his own joke.

"Nope, between the trees in the wooded area that skirts your fields," I said. "You've got pot plants all through the trees. So many of them that you guard the area at night. I spotted your hammock out there. Seems like an awfully strange place to want to chow down on fast food and take a nap, don't you think? It does seem like a good place to post a guard, though, just in case the wrong people were to wander into your other crop."

"You don't know nothin'."

"I know about the pot, but what I don't know about is Hunter Grayson's notebook. What made it so valuable to you?"

"You think you're pretty smart. But then again, so did Grayson. He writes in his little book. 'In the glen there is a secret, one I cannot, will not tell.' Bonnet Farm was the secret he would not tell – for money that is. He showed up every month to collect his rent for Miss Libby. Old British hippy with his little gray ponytail. He found out we were growing pot and insisted on more rent money and a steady supply of weed to help him to 'forget.'"

Allison stepped further into the light and took Danny by the elbow. "That's why we had to make him forget permanently." As she lifted it toward us, her pink Hello Kitty watched sparkled in the light. I knew then that it had been the sparkle I kept seeing. "When that old fool Simmons started hollering about Charlie Loper, it was just so much easier," she said. "You got in the way, finding the only proof of our arrangement, and I had to take you out. We broke into the museum and stole Charlie Loper's guns and then just let the town do the talking."

"You had to take me out? Why not have Coop do it?"

"Because Coop, although good for some things," she smiled knowingly, "is a piss-poor shot. Growing up in Texas and attending the finest schools, you can bet my daddy made sure I spent some time at the shooting range. Just part of a good Texas education."

I was still confused as to why a girl with all of the advantages she had received in life would pair up with someone like Coop. Coop was at the other end of the economic spectrum, the kind of boy you didn't want to introduce to your parents. It seemed that Allison had the classic bad-boy crush, and it had driven her to murder.

"Allison, you have everything you could ever want," I said. "Why would you risk it all with a man like Coop?"

"That's what you think. That's what everybody thinks," she said. "Sure, I had money, schools, vacations, stuff ...but I never had a mom and dad who would take the time to be with me. They were always off somewhere, or if they were home, they sent me off somewhere. I had the best childhood money could buy, but my parents weren't parents. They were what I called my principal investors."

"And you saw great parenting in the Bonnets?"

"What I saw was a family that stuck together, no matter what. Clay Bonnet would kill for his son. My dad would never do anything like that."

"What about Dr. Springer? Was she in on it too?" I asked.

"No and yes. I told her we'd play a joke on the town and dress like Charlie Loper at the pet parade. Everyone was so nervous anyway, so I told her it was a way to calm the town down. It was all going to be a big joke and then we'd come out in our costumes and award the winner. It made a great cover for me to get a chance to take a shot at you in broad daylight. Then I let Coop here take the shot instead, and he hit Noodles the poodle."

"I told you the gun wouldn't fire right from that far," he whined.

"Man, was Dr. Springer surprised. She stepped out, just like we planned, but when she saw everyone down there running from the attack, she turned and ran. I have to say, killing her was harder than I thought it would be. I mean, look at all those poor animals who have to find a new doctor. Pretty thoughtless of me, don't you think? I caught up with her back at the office. That's where I shot her."

"So you thought the town would think that she was playing the ghost of Charlie Loper, but it didn't last."

"Coop and I moved her body behind Earl's during the night. She became our cover." I nodded, realizing Allison and Coop didn't know Dr. Springer was still alive.

"Betsy, can we go home now?" Danny asked. He leaned over to Allison, who was still holding the Colt 45.

"You're not supposed to play with guns, Allison," he said. "They hurt people, you know."

"Oh, yes I do very much, Danny. But don't worry. I've learned that with this old gun, from this distance I'm a pretty good shot. You won't feel a thing."

Danny shifted on his feet and started pulling my arm. Allison lifted her arm to shoot, and I decided maybe Danny had a pretty good idea. I pulled him to the wood floor of the gazebo to get him out of the line of fire – no easy task for someone who outweighed me. As we hit the ground I heard a scream, and I looked up to see Allison holding on to her arm and dropping the pistol to the ground as she slipped down the steps. Blood was gushing out of her wrist.

On the other side of the gazebo, Clay Bonnet held a Glock semi-automatic pistol.

"You stupid girl. You had to go and save us. Don't you understand? This here's a family operation – and you ain't a part of the family."

"Shut up, daddy," Coop said as he held Allison in his arms. "Allison's going to be my wife. You got no call to speak to her that way."

"She's a murdering, scheming woman, Coop, and she's the one who's gonna end up putting us all in jail."

I pulled Danny out of the gazebo. I was sure Clay Bonnet's next bullet would be for me, but he didn't shoot.

He swerved with his gun pointed in our direction. "Stop right there, Happy Hinter," he said. "I might be a drug dealer, but I sure as hell don't murder people."

I drew in a breath, feeling my heart pound in my chest. I would have to strike that off my list of assumptions. Not all drug dealers are murderers. Not all drug dealers are murderers.

Chapter 28

From across the park, I could see a crowd running toward us. Elena ran up to Allison, kicking her gun away from her on the ground. She called for an ambulance on her cell phone. George drew his gun on Clay Bonnet, who responded by removing the magazine from his gun. Bonnet racked the slide to remove a remaining bullet and then placed the gun on the ground. He backed away and reached for a piece of paper out of his wallet. Coop quickly changed allegiances and stood over by his dad.

"I think we've found your murderer here, Officer. Here's my concealed carry permit." Clay Bonnet handed George a small card. "I shot her in the nick of time. She was about to take two more victims."

George took the card and flicked on a flashlight to read it. "Well, Mr. Bonnet, looks like you're a hero."

"No, no, not a hero. Just trying to protect my son, here." He put his arm around Coop.

Elena turned to me and Danny. "Are you two all right?"

"Yes," Danny said.

"We're fine, but there's more to the story than what Mr. Bonnet is telling you," I began.

"Would that involve that extra crop he's been growing in the woods on his land?" I didn't even realize my father was behind us.

"I don't know what you're talking about," Clay Bonnet said. "Besides that, you're under investigation for trying to frame me."

"The thing is," Adam stepped up from behind my dad. "If we were to get a subpoena to do a little digging out there, what do you think we might find?"

"Watermelons," Coop growled.

"And a whole lot more, I'm thinkin'."

"Get a subpoena," Clay challenged.

"Not a problem. I think I can persuade the judge pretty easily at this point." Adam smiled at Elena.

The entire fireworks crowd seemed to be closing in on the dark end of the park. In the front stood Leo and the boys. Seeing Aunt Maggie, Danny got up and ran to her.

"Miss Allison's hurt, Mama."

"I'm so sorry, baby. Did they call an ambulance?"

"Yes."

"Then she'll be okay then. Don't you worry." Maggie hugged Danny, stroking his straight brown hair.

"I thought you were heading to the dump?" I said.

"I sent Howard on. Something pulled me back." Aunt Maggie admitted.

Leo motioned for the boys to stay with the crowd and walked over and helped me up.

"Damn girl, you're in trouble again," he said, shaking his head.

"I guess you're right. I am a hard person to be involved with. It just seems like everything is going along fine and the next thing I know, I'm mixed up in something and ..."

"I get it. I get it. You're Nancy Drew, Miss Marple and MacGyver all put together – but what does that make me?"

"I can help on that one." My father held up his hand.

"Hush, Dad." I turned to Leo. "I just wanted to let you know that if it's all too much for you ... I understand."

Leo sighed and ran his fingers through his hair. He chewed on his lower lip and then lowered himself down on one knee.

Had I dropped something down there? The thing was, he didn't seem to be searching for anything. His eyes were on me. I suddenly figured out what he was intending to do and was filled with more terror than I had felt after confronting not one, not two, but three killers.

"Betsy?" He reached into his jeans pocket and pulled out a little black box. How had I not felt that earlier?

"Betsy!" he repeated. I pulled my attention back to him.

"Yes," I said, finding my voice shaky.

"I don't know where our life will take us. Seeing as I'm proposing at a crime scene, I'm counting on it being pretty interesting. I know you were hurt badly before, but I also know I can't imagine my life without you in it. From the minute my kid knocked your kid down at the Scout meeting and I thought you were going to slug me, it was love at first sight. I know this is a strange time to ask you, but Betsy..."

A tear rolled down my cheek. After all that we had been through, he still felt this way?

"Betsy, will you marry me?"

I opened my mouth to speak and heard the crowd behind us shouting, "Yes! Yes! Yes!"

We both laughed, and then I uttered a single word.

"Yes."

Leo stood up, encased me in a giant hug and then lowered his lips to mine just as a fireworks blossom went off above us in the Texas sky. From behind us I heard more cheers. As I put on my new engagement ring, I noticed the light hit it – and it sparkled. It was by far the prettiest sparkle tonight in Pecan Bayou, and I was pretty glad it wasn't followed by gunfire.

Chapter 29

"Cousin Leo! I have a Cousin Leo!" Danny said as we all raised a glass on my front porch in the moonlight. I sipped at my champagne and gazed over at Leo. The boys were out on the front lawn chasing after fireflies. Leo and Tyler had stayed the weekend, and my father spent most of Sunday dealing with his newest visitors in the Pecan Bayou jail.

"You surprised us all there, Leo. We never expected you to propose." Maggie patted him on the shoulder.

"In the middle of a pot bust," Dad said.

"In the middle of catching a killer," I added.

"Well, there never seemed to be the right time with you people. I had to move when Betsy was standing still and not being shot at."

I reached over and ran my hand along his cheek. "Thanks for working with me."

Dad set down his glass and put his hands behind his head and stretched. "Once we got Coop Bonnet down to the station, he started talkin'. Seems he's not such a tough guy when he's facing a prison sentence. Told us Allison was the driving force behind all of it."

"Now you know his daddy isn't going to let him take all the heat," Maggie said.

"His daddy is facing some heat of his own. Adam got over there with the subpoena, and they found enough pot in the trees to supply another Woodstock. He's looking at a marijuana cultivation conviction with a sentence of two to twenty years, we figure."

"What about Lina?" I said.

Dad took off his glasses and rubbed his eyes. "From all that we can tell, Lina was in on it but never took part in any of the business side. It was her job to manage the legal part of the farm. If the judge gives her anything, it'll probably just be a fine."

"So will she stay on out there?" Leo asked.

"No, she said she can't manage it without her husband and son – but here's the kicker, Libby is moving out there."

Maggie laughed. "Libby? The poor little rich girl?"

"Yep. She's taking over the farm and with the help of some hired hands will be running it. She is also moving the Charlie Loper museum out there. It will be Pecan Bayou's newest tourist attraction."

"That's good to hear. This might be just the thing Miss Libby needs to make her happy," I said.

"That is, if she makes sure she hires good people," Leo added.

"I've already suggested she do a background check on anyone she puts in her employ," said my dad.

"Is Dr. Springer better?" Danny asked.

"I called the hospital this afternoon, Danny," Maggie said, "and she came out of her coma. The doctors say she will make a full recovery. Your boss is going to be all right. Probably the best part of all of that is she's talking. She's already said she'll be glad to testify against Allison and Coop."

"She's another one who needs to do a background check on her help," I said.

"Yes, well, Allison's parents are on their way. They were out of the country, of course, and have already warned Chief Wilson that they are hiring the finest lawyer money can buy," Dad said.

Leo reached over and squeezed my knee. "Lawyer or no, it's pretty hard to get out of a murder and attempted murder."

"I still don't get how a girl who has everything could do something like that," Maggie said.

"Oh, she had everything, but the one thing she wanted her parents couldn't buy." I looked out at the boys now lying down on the lawn, looking up at the stars in the Texas summer sky.

"Well, I guess she has her parents' attention now, doesn't she?" Dad said, and then he leaned over and patted Leo on the back. "So, now that you're engaged, where do you think you're going to live?"

"Dallas," Leo said – at the same time I said, "Pecan Bayou."

"Betsy, I'm a meteorologist, and my office is in Dallas," he protested.

"You are in hurricane country, Leo. You can work anywhere," I answered.

"Okay you two," my father said. "You have a few things to work out. In the meantime, a toast – to two of the most mismatched and most in love people I've ever met." We all raised our glasses, and I clinked my against Leo's. Butch jumped up between us and planted puppy kisses on my face.

"Hey, boy, that's my job!" said Leo.

"It sure is," I said and planted my own kiss on my brand new fiancé.

Helpful Hints from the Happy Hinter

There are thousands of pets available for adoption every day in the United States. If you choose to adopt and provide a home for a puppy like Butch, here are few things to keep in mind:

• Investigate the breed of the dog you are thinking about adopting. This will help you make decisions about temperament and maintenance.

• Make sure you have food and water bowls, toys, collar and leash.

• Figure out the household rules for the dog before he gets in the door. Will he be allowed on the furniture? Will he get scraps from the table? Who will walk and train the dog?

• Just like if you brought home a new baby, you'll want to make sure there is nothing on the floor or anything that the dog can ingest that is dangerous to him. Be sure to provide plenty of toys for chewing if you have a new puppy.

• Make an appointment with your veterinarian for the pet to have a thorough exam. Make sure the dog's shots are all up to date, and consider spaying or neutering.

• Be prepared to spend time with your pet playing and helping it to feel at home in your home.

How to Clean Paving Stones (like the blood-stained ones around Charlie Loper's fountain)

1. Sweep away any dirt and debris on the stones and then spray the area with water from the hose.

2. Cover any grass or plants that might come in contact with the cleaning formula. You can use a drop cloth or something like an old shower curtain.

3. Make a solution of half bleach/half warm water and pour it on the affected area, being careful not to touch any surrounding greenery.

4. Scrub the area with a long-handled brush and then hose it down with water again.

Recipes

Berry Watermelon Smoothie
Ingredients
1/4 watermelon
125 g frozen mixed berries or 125 g fresh mixed berries
1 or 2 bananas
1/4-1/2 cup milk (optional – soy or rice milk works too, or use any juice as a substitute)
ice (optional)
cinnamon
honey
Directions
Blend watermelon into a juice.
Add bananas (use mainly to thicken).
Throw in other ingredients, all according to taste.

Watermelon Lemonade
Mix together these ingredients.
6 cups watermelon
1 cup water
1/3 cup sugar
1/2 cup lemon juice

Peanut Butter Pie from the Pecan Bayou Diner
Ingredients
1 (8-ounce) package cream cheese
1 1/2 cups confectioners' sugar
1 cup peanut butter
1 cup milk
1 (16-ounce) package frozen whipped topping, thawed
2 (9-inch) prepared graham cracker crusts
Directions
1. Beat together cream cheese and confectioners' sugar. Mix in peanut butter and milk. Beat until smooth. Fold in whipped topping.

2. Spoon the mixture into two 9-inch graham cracker pie shells. Cover and freeze until firm.

Aunt Maggie's Yo-Yo Pattern

Cut out a circle of fabric. You can use the bottom of any jar for a template, depending on how big of a yo-yo you want to make. Just remember you will be gathering the yo-yo, so don't make it too small. A regular-sized peanut butter jar or bigger is a good size.

Once you get your yo-yo cut out, heat up the iron and press a 1/ 4-inch seam all the way around the circle of fabric.

Sew a running stitch all the way around your seam using small, even stitches. Do not backstitch. You want to be able to gather the stitch when you finish.

Pull the thread tight. It will make a much smaller circle with a hole in the middle. Tie it off with two small stitches and a knot.

Flatten your completed yo-yo with your hand so that the hole is centered.

When you have several yo-yos, you can sew them together to create a quilt top, a pillow – or even a costume for a dog in a parade.

Helping Dogs Handle the Noise of Fireworks

Many dogs are frightened of fireworks. There are many ways you can get your favorite pooch through this stressful time. You may want to try and desensitize your dog to the sound of the fireworks. They can listen to a video or recording featuring fireworks to try to accustom them to the sound. Gradually turn the volume up – but if your dog becomes fearful, turn it back down. You may need to do this several times. You can also reward your dog with a treat for sitting calmly while listening.

Lavonne's Homemade Window Cleaner

Mix equal parts of water and vinegar. Because there is no rubbing alcohol in this recipe, it will take longer to dry. Use a microfiber cloth to clean the glass. It will make a difference on all your museum cases!

About the Author

Teresa Trent writes cozy mysteries that take place in small towns in Texas. She was born in Chattanooga, Tennessee but with her father in the military, didn't stay for long. She's lived all over but has a special place in her heart for Colorado, Illinois and of course, Texas. Being a fan of the Andy Griffith Show and Murder She Wrote she loves creating quirky small towns and colorful characters. She decided to feature a character with Down syndrome in the Pecan Bayou series because after giving birth to her son with DS, she discovered there were very few people like him in the world of cozy mysteries. She continues that with the character of Gigi, a young woman with cerebral palsy in the Henry Park Series. Teresa lives in Houston, Texas with her husband, two of her adult children and a needy dachshund mix named Martin Luther.

Series by Teresa Trent

Acknowledgments

Thank you to Rachel for helping me once again. Your assistance is invaluable. Thank you to Susan for your help on the book and sharing your experiences with weimaraners. Thank you to my husband for his information about Colt 45s and for always supporting me in my writing.

Don't miss out!

Visit the website below and you can sign up to receive emails whenever Teresa Trent publishes a new book. There's no charge and no obligation.

https://books2read.com/r/B-A-FJQD-UVDO

Connecting independent readers to independent writers.

www.ingramcontent.com/pod-product-compliance
Lightning Source LLC
Chambersburg PA
CBHW021011180626
46814CB00003B/1244